$4.50

"This novel is permeated with atmosphere—full of a foreboding in which events roll mysteriously, but inevitably, to a grim conclusion."   —*Library Journal*

"It's David Lynch turf."   —*San Jose Mercury-News*

"Well crafted . . . eerily evil . . . yields a sexually explicit erotic edge."   —*Publishers Weekly*

"Told in a masterful gothic style."   —*Lambda Book Report*

"An unusually disturbing first novel. This would make a truly scary movie: Are you listening, Polanski?"   —*Kirkus Reviews*

"A thrilling melange of hallucinations, fantasies, and murder."   —*Chattanooga Times*

T. L. PARKINSON lives in San Francisco. *The Man Upstairs* is his first novel.

THE MAN UPSTAIRS

by T. L. Parkinson

A PLUME BOOK

PLUME
Published by the Penguin Group
Penguin Books USA Inc., 375 Hudson Street, New York, New York 10014, U.S.A.
Penguin Books Ltd, 27 Wrights Lane, London W8 5TZ, England
Penguin Books Australia Ltd, Ringwood, Victoria, Australia
Penguin Books Canada Ltd, 10 Alcorn Avenue, Toronto, Ontario, Canada M4V 3B2
Penguin Books (N.Z.) Ltd, 182-190 Wairau Road, Auckland 10, New Zealand

Penguin Books Ltd, Registered Offices: Harmondsworth, Middlesex, England

Published by Plume, an imprint of New American Library, a division of Penguin Books USA Inc.
Previously published in a Dutton edition.

First Plume Printing, October, 1992
10 9 8 7 6 5 4 3 2 1

 REGISTERED TRADEMARK—MARCA REGISTRADA

LIBRARY OF CONGRESS CATALOGING-IN-PUBLICATION DATA
Parkinson, T. L.
     The man upstairs / T. L. Parkinson.
     p.   cm.
     ISBN 0-452-26847-8
     I. Title.
     [PS3566.A6897M36   1992]
     813'.54—dc20   92-53560
                                                     CIP

Printed in the United States of America

To Kay McCauley

Many thanks to Chris Schelling and Brandy Leigh Mow
for invaluable editorial assistance
and moral support

With dusk begins to cry
the male of the Waiting-insect—
I, too, await my beloved,
and, hearing, my longing grows.

TSURAYUKI, *Kokinshu*
(A.D. 905)

Outside in the street, dogs were fighting.

I hesitated at the door. The world out there seemed huge and threatening. I reminded myself that I had only to follow the thread—from my old apartment to the new one, barely a mile away—and I would be safe inside again.

It was almost midnight. I had left an old clock on the mantel above the stone fireplace that had always leaked smoke. The ticking in the nearly empty room was louder than gunfire. Soon that measured violence would lead us to the witching hour.

I closed the door and went down the stairs. The dog and cat were already in the car. Although I hadn't been happy here, I felt a moment of unreasonable nostalgia and fought the urge to go back up.

It was a windless Halloween night. Jake was in the back seat, his big black nose smearing the glass. The cat must have been hiding under the endless odds and ends the movers didn't take, which had looked like nothing but which filled the car to bursting. Still, we had to leave stuff behind.

I would not return to clean it out, however; let that be my revenge against the landlord who had evicted me.

There was no air in the cramped car. I kept the windows tightly closed; the car was me. Everything was me. Jake needed a walk, the cat was plowing through boxes one minute, screeching with terror the next.

At Market Street I got snarled in a traffic jam. I felt foolish, no more important than any of the flotsam that floated through my sight. We must look out of place, I thought, and I know the discomfort shows on my face. An old child, that is how I look; a child that has cried for hours unheard, and has now cried itself dry.

Masked people thronged, jostled, through the steam curtain of my breath. No one seemed to notice me. Didn't anyone sense my predicament? The humor and the pathos?

Dared I hope for a savior?

A man carrying a wand and wearing silver Jockey shorts approached the closed window. I rolled it down, without thinking. Was he about to ask for help? Or offering me help? I smiled.

Noticing my noticing, he lurched away like a creature with faulty wiring. He cast a disdainful glance over his shoulder, as though I had broken some unspoken rule.

A Bride of Frankenstein walked by, without an escort. There were several Bette Davises and Marilyn Monroes, a group of young men wearing nylons pulled over their faces, ghouls with knives sticking out of their foreheads, vampires with blood dripping from bruised lips. A flock of small children dressed as nightmare creatures, the kind children imagine lurk under their beds.

The usual.

Finally the light changed. On and on they came, in waves, masked, caped, crawling, an army of them, blocking traffic.

The car in front was packed with teenagers—turned-up collars, hair teased and too long, or greased back, necks arched in aggression. Looking for trouble.

I nudged my car forward, hoping they'd get the idea. Use some of that aggression to get us out of here.

The light changed from green to red and back again. Still no movement.

Then something shot past my ear. I reached out instinctively to protect myself, and then tried to grab that something when I realized what had happened.

My cat had jumped out the window, which I had rolled down only six inches to greet the man with the wand.

I pulled the car over quickly, scattering celebrants. A couple of people gave me the finger. Masked people stumbled, my brakes screeched. I flung open the door. It seemed for a moment that the crowd would come after me—I could sense the hive mind trying to focus its hostility—but suddenly the tide swept them out and away.

I saw my cat scuttle under a group of wraiths dragging black chains. I ran into the center of the group, the wind from my passing setting the chains dancing in the air—they were black construction paper.

My cat's tail flicked finally, then he was gone—swallowed up, over there, impossibly far away.

"My cat," I whined to a passing drag queen. "He ran under there." I gestured helplessly.

"What am I supposed to do, buddy?" Behind the mascara there was something human—perhaps he had a cat too. Stay and help me, I thought.

A skinny Chicano kid with shiny black hair leered at me. Apparently anyone talking to a drag queen was a target. I hardened my face, bit my tongue, and moved on.

The kid found someone else—an ugly man in a dress— crooked nose, two days' growth of beard, broad hairy shoulders sprouting like unlikely wings from his black evening gown.

The kid gathered spit in his mouth.

The man in the dress swung around quickly and spit in the kid's face. "Gotta be fast if you're going to make it . . . sonny."

"Cocksucking faggot," the kid screamed, jumping up and down in the same spot. He wiped his face. He looked like he was going to cry.

I went back to my car. I had left the keys in the ignition.

I'd come back tomorrow and post signs: "LOST CAT," and a Xerox of the one photo I had of him, a generic kitten picture. What else could I do?

By the time I got up the palm-lined street to my new

place, I was pounding the wheel, laughing, crying, hot tears flying from my face and splashing my hands.

I had been forced out of a large inexpensive place into this: a one-bedroom apartment with a big tree out back that blocked the sun, low ceilings, a kitchen that looked into a dark well.

The building had eight units. Built in the thirties, it had been refurbished many times, according to the tides of fashion. Scar tissue? The apartments seemed sheathed in it.

The brick facade was painted brick color, aluminum bay windows rattled constantly even in the mildest breeze. Above the foyer were grinning children's faces painted gaudy colors; the paint was chipping, and one of the faces had unpainted wooden eyes, which seemed to stare at me when I passed: blank, dull, yet intense in their scrutiny.

Inside, there was a theatrical carpet—Mexican art deco, if there is such a thing. The doors to the apartments were glass, with gray industrial shades inside, thick enough to block the light from an exploding sun.

My place was on the second floor in the back. If I looked through the millions of tiny leaves that battered my fake bay window, I could see the L-shaped swimming pool, the gazebo, some wilting yellow roses, and a giant palm tree (said to be the largest of its kind in Northern California) that stood directly opposite the tree that blocked my view, circumscribing the yard with branches and shadows of branches.

Turning about in the empty rooms, I thought: This is my new home.

For two days I stayed inside mostly, trying to get the place to resonate. I kept the lights dim; dim yellow light seemed homey. It didn't work. I hung pictures in what should have been just the right places. I tried to arrange the furniture the way it had been before. It had been perfect. Now everything was cumbersome, too large or too small, and I kept stumbling over things.

Stubbornly, the past would not let itself be duplicated.

When I had finished arranging things—it took days, and three headaches—no echo of the past remained. My new place had a will of its own. My green chair looked blue; the plants were huge, out of place—I cut them back until there was nothing left. The desk that had fitted into that other little nook now occupied a whole wall, where I had thought to put an aquarium.

I was so absorbed by my interior design that I was only dimly aware of sounds from other apartments. An occasional knocking, from up or down I could not tell, dull roars that might be planes or cars or bombs. They did not deter me from my manic nest building. These were hollow sounds, the evidence of a distant war. I hoped the front would move on and leave me behind in peace.

Finally the arrangement seemed tolerable. The apartment didn't feel right exactly—but there was a sense of inevitability about where things belonged. Eventually I relented to the pattern that had slowly, persistently unfolded.

On the third night of my new occupancy, the fire alarm went off at three A.M. I woke up in a panic, throwing off the covers. The glowing face of the clock was the first thing I saw. I felt my head, because it seemed someone had pushed a knife through it. My body was beaded with cold sweat. I slid across the resinous hardwood floor to the front door. Jake chased me, growling lowly. I must have looked the part of the madman, hair matted, eyes bulging, my pajama bottoms half falling off, as I rushed into the hall and down the stairs.

In the foyer the sound was deafening, blinding. I held my hands over my ears. No one else had come out of their apartment. The red alarm bells were shrieking to a deaf audience. Could everyone be away, on vacation, at after-hours clubs? No, I had heard my neighbors earlier this evening.

But what kind of people could sleep through this? Would a real war, which would have been no louder, waken them? I shivered, not looking forward to finding out.

I stared dumbly at the red box that held the switches for the building's electrical system. The key was around here somewhere—the landlord had showed me where when I had signed the rental agreement, but my head wasn't working right. The sound blasted away any thoughts or memories as soon as they were formed.

It was a full five minutes before the other tenants came down. I stood there waiting. The sound seemed to crescendo, then to diminish. By the time they came down the stairs—wearing bathrobes, faces wrinkled like babies, shadowed eyes, looking bored and petulant—the constancy of the shrill had begun to resemble silence.

"Oh, we're used to it," a sleep-tossed creature said. Then he or she got the key from the window ledge and turned off the alarm. Its sudden absence sank through me like nausea. I was looking at the front door, resisting an impulse to run screaming into the street.

I watched their reflections in the front glass as they disappeared back up the stairs.

The place was a plague of mirrors. At the back of the quaint china cabinets, at the end of the dark hall, a full mirror of wavy glass in the bathroom, three segmented ones in the kitchen (someone's idea of art—I intended to pry them out), and a scarred mirror on the closet door next to my bed, tall as a grown man.

This last one was my favorite, because I could lie in bed thinking, listening to the whispering of the building, and look up to see what feeling had crawled onto my face. I would talk to myself as though I were my ex-wife, trying to cajole the feeling from my face.

I open up slowly, I said to my face. I have my own time-table. My ex-wife would have said I never opened up. She called me her false promise, just like her father. Michael, I said, Michael, you've got to get a grip on yourself. Sometimes my voice was high, sometimes low.

I could make the image of my face do anything I wanted. At least that was something. I felt like a filmmaker. Blond hair, full lips, and dark green eyes (when they weren't squinting), infinitely malleable. I could be dog tired, blood-hound mournful. Handsome, glazed eyes looking ominously from under thick lashes. I could stand, and stick out my belly like a child's; force my muscles forward and downward, defining an athletic body.

I could almost hear Dorothy's voice. "Michael," she

would say and I said now, "I thought you were looking at me. But you're looking at yourself—your favorite subject."

I was trying to put myself back together, to reassemble a broken mirror about a human spine.

One night, as I continued the attempted integration, the doorbell rang. Jake went berserk. I groped in the dark for the hall light, found strange bumpy paneling, but no switch.

I opened the door slowly, choking on the musty close air in the windowless hall.

Light waltzed in. It was like a summer breeze, a phantom of sunlight shooting down between storm clouds. In the middle of it—defining it—was Janette, as tall as a man, dressed in a pink silk blouse, strand of creamy pearls, sandy hair artfully tossed. She had a genuinely warm smile on her face.

Surprise, a person, come knocking. You don't have to go out after all.

"My God," Janette (upstairs, front right) said, handing me a spectacular flower arrangement—there were so many intense colors, my eyes couldn't focus. Not something I would have selected. "Have you got a dog or what?" she said, looking down at Jake, who was lying across my feet. He had been barking ferociously when the doorbell rang. "Will it eat me?" she said coyly. British, I thought, lower-middle-class, aspires to better.

"Oh, are these for me?" I said.

"Does someone else live here?" While I smelled the flowers, she produced a bottle of champagne she had been holding behind her.

I stood in the dark hallway and caught my breath.

"Come in," I said. "We shouldn't stand here in the dark."

She pushed gently past me. "If you will show me to your kitchen," she said, "I'll get things ready."

I pointed. "To the right and around the corner. You can't miss it. If you turn around inside here, you're everywhere."

"Strange," she said, not insincerely but sounding unaffected. "Your apartment is the exact opposite of mine."

"Welcome to the mirror world," I said.

I had run into her in the hall once or twice, after the incident with the alarm. Gregarious, charming, hard to figure. She seemed overly zealous, so I had not encouraged her.

Yet, here she was.

"I thought you might be feeling lonely," she said. The sound of another human voice flushed the walls. It was as if someone had turned up the lights. "The people in this building are snooty at first. They're terribly depressed. We all are," she laughed. "But I'm not."

Janette found the glasses and the ice bucket without my help.

"Industrious, aren't you?" I said from the kitchen door, where I stood like a diver ready to dive into a pool of light. It felt nice to have someone else going through my cupboards.

"Well, a girl can't sit around waiting for things to happen. Besides, I like nosing about in other people's apartments. Have anything interesting in your medicine cabinet? You better take it out if you do. I read people's souls by the contents of their medicine cabinets."

I smiled. My medicine cabinet was probably empty.

"I hate waiting too," I said. "I was waiting when you knocked. For something. Maybe you." Sounded like bar talk. I immediately regretted it. "Well, for something."

She seemed pleased nevertheless. "Oh, you charmer," she said. "I love an insincere man. But you're sad, I can see that. I don't mean to embarrass you. I arrived just in the nick of time. You'll feel better when you've had some of this"—she held the bottle between her breasts. "Moving is one of the four things that can really throw you off. The other three being a loved one dying, losing a job, and illness."

"You read self-help books?" I said.

"No, it's common knowledge," she said. "Those idiots get paid to tell imbeciles what the caveman knew. They call it civilization." She handed me the ice bucket, now full of ice. "Why don't you set this up in the living room? Then we can have a proper celebration."

And we did have a proper celebration. The next morning, when I awoke, she had pinned a note to my pillow:

"Sorry I couldn't wait for you to wake. Waiting, you know, against nature." (She had forgotten the "my.")

She signed it with a heart with an arrow piercing it, followed by two J's looped together.

All day, as I pored over the billing forms at the hospital (Department of Psychiatry, Mount Zion Hospital), I kept trying to imagine Janette's face, and could not.

My own face kept popping into my mind instead.

Had we used condoms? The ones I had were old, at least six months. A fatal admission for a man. Had Janette brought her own? (This seemed likely.) Did we have a good time? Had I been a considerate lover? Was she the type to kiss and tell? Would I be the talk of the building?

It was all a blank.

"Listen, really, Michael is so nice—but he came so fast he made my head spin. I had to finish myself. He was drunk and passed out before I had barely begun."

I could not remember anything after the first sip of champagne. Janette's note had been polite enough. Didn't that indicate at least an adequate time? Yet a cloudy apprehension would not leave me.

Odd, but when I looked inside myself, where the memory of last night should have been, it was like staring at a blank wall.

I watched my face reflected in my coffee—rippling, dark, irritable, unshaven, and behind me a light glowing ominously, like an underwater sun.

"So, Michael," I said to my floating, hung-over self, "what do you think happened?"

After work, I took Jake to Golden Gate Park for a run, and got a ticket for having an unleashed dog. I smiled at the officer, trying to make a joke. "I can never find those strips of parkland where dogs are allowed to run," I said to the unsmiling, overweight woman. "There are three of them, right?"

"Yep," she said, handing me the ticket and staring at the ground like a morose child.

"Come on, Jake," I said, throwing the ticket on the ground as soon as the police car was out of sight, "might as well go home and face the music."

I drove back through the park, thinking about Janette, and the likelihood that we would have an awkward moment. There were black buffalo in a bare fenced field, pretty green lawns that stretched into the misty distances, clusters of palm trees surrounding inner lagoons: an intense unnatural green radiation.

A sprinkling system kept it alive during the dry months, which with the passing years seemed to be stretching. Little in the park was indigenous. If the park depended on the sky, much of it would look like the straw-colored pit where they kept the buffalo.

I drove as slowly as I could, until cars started to honk. I must be going backward: it takes a lot to get sleepy Californians to honk their horns.

When I got to my block, Janette was pulling up in her yellow sports car. Perfect timing. Well, let's get it over with quickly, then we can get on with things.

I found a space in front of the building. A good omen. The sun shining from the front door was blinding, an eye into a white inferno. Janette scowled as she parked half a block away; she had apparently been eyeing my space.

I pulled my papers together, which had fallen to the floor, and slowly got out of the car. I could dash inside, on one pretense or other, avoid a confrontation.

Post-whatever is so awkward. But it appeared ducking inside would only make things worse.

A large ugly man unfolded from Janette's tiny yellow car. At first I thought he was a tree shadow. I was amazed that such a large man could fit inside the compact car.

He walked around and opened the door for Janette. She took his hand and they walked casually to where I waited by the curb.

"Michael," she said, giving me a hug while retaining hold of the arm of the hook-nosed man, who looked like an Aztec warrior, "this is my boss, Fred Feretti."

I shook his strong dry hand.

"Fred's a doctor, a neurologist. I work in the office. I told you last night. You probably don't remember." Fred had a broad chest and nipples which threatened to tear through the fabric of his tight-fitting knit shirt. I tried not to look.

"Michael works in a hospital too," she said. I looked for tension or discomfort in her voice, but found none. She was as featureless as burnished steel, cool clear to the center. Fred coughed nervously while staring at me with penetrating olive-colored eyes. No one said anything for a couple dozen seconds.

"Upstairs, now," Janette said when the silence became threatening, and pointed a tanned finger with calm authority. I felt a vague admiration for her impeccable timing. "I'll show you the brochures for the new office furniture."

"Nice to meet you . . . Fred." I said his name with difficulty. The sound of my own voice surprised me. Janette looked at me quizzically; then the warm smile returned.

"The same," Fred said. They walked toward the front door. Fred was about to open the door, but Janette beat him to it.

"Inside," she said.

I've always liked swimming pools. We had one when I was a kid. There is something romantic about all that contained water. I counted myself lucky to live in a building that had one. There weren't many in the city.

It was unfilled now, and being resurfaced. The bluish-white insides were puckered, peeling. I dangled my legs into the empty air, imagining water.

I told myself that maybe when the pool was repainted-

and filled, then I would feel comfortable in my new home. It was a friendly metaphor, and made my stomach feel warm.

As I stared into the empty cavity—which somehow reminded me of an inverted building—I detected movement, a flicker of shadow, at the other end of the yard, under the big palm tree. I looked up. The shadow opened like a knife into the figure of a woman.

The young woman, another neighbor, made a strange muted sound, which might have been "hello," and then, with quick small steps, made her way into the shadows. The back gate opened and closed.

The gate banged in the wind. The hinge was loose and it took some work to fasten the gate tight. I walked to the gate and fastened it. You needn't have run, I thought. I've often seen you from my window, staring into the empty pool, conjuring water.

I felt a strange exhilaration, as though I had stumbled onto another's private fantasy world. A world not unlike mine own, perhaps. I hoped I hadn't usurped her territory.

I sat by the pool awhile longer. The sky got dark and blood-red clouds moved across the sky. The sun sank into the rooftops, sending up a faint shimmer from the tarpaper, like stardust.

The evening wind came up suddenly, stirring the trees.

Then the dizzying scent of late-blooming flowers drove me back inside my apartment.

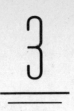

"**Y**ou've got to do something about it," I said, whining a little. My landlord was a fierce Italian with a grizzled red face. I should have known better than to challenge him outright.

"You've just moved in and you have one problem after another. First the refrigerator wasn't cold enough, then you wanted a light in the closet. Then the fire alarm bothered you. Now it's the Fergusons. Understand me, I don't have any great liking for them ..." He stopped himself, looked perturbed, as though he had revealed a guilty secret. "It's your word against theirs," he said suddenly, shifting gears. "You'll have to work it out between you."

"I have a right to a peaceful home," I mumbled as the landlord stormed down the stairs.

Patricia, who lived across the hall from me, had come out and quietly observed the encounter. She was the girl who watched the empty pool at twilight. "Oh, he'll ask the Fergusons to quiet down—and be more tolerant. They're quite a schizy couple." She backed against her door, keeping one hand inside. "Sorry, I couldn't help overhearing."

"That's all right, we were making quite a racket. Not as loud as the Fergusons, who seem to throw furniture instead of talking." I smiled. "Honestly, though, if I make a move, they are down here asking me to keep quiet. Double standard, to say the least. I feel like I'm living with my parents again."

"Did your parents fight?" Patricia asked. She came out into the hall light. She had green eyes, a slender neck, pale long fingers. "They're junkies . . . or at least I think so."

I looked up. "You mean there is a *reason?* It isn't me?" I laughed, and then she laughed too, deeply, from the center of her chest.

"They've been carrying on like that since I've been here—and I've lived here for almost, let's see, three years now." She held a translucent finger to her chin thoughtfully; the curve was like a tender flower stalk.

Upstairs, thunder. We looked up, at each other, suppressing a smile. The Fergusons roared down the stairs, past us, screaming obscenities. Hostile, impersonal, perfectly timed.

"We're invisible, apparently," I said. "This can't be real life."

"See what I mean? It isn't you, it isn't me. It's . . . something else," Patricia said, shaking her head as if to rid it of the unpleasantness. "I do feel sorry for you having to live under . . . that." She pointed to the trail the domestic fire had left in the air; I could almost see it as her hand traced it.

"Like living inside a drum," I replied, looking up. Patricia grimaced. I hoped my mood didn't show on my face. When I felt bad, I looked like a serial killer.

"Maybe I should go enjoy the silence while they're out."

"Okay," she said. "See you again soon. I saw you out back the other day, but I was getting into a role. I'm an actress. I hope you weren't offended. When I'm working, I'm standoffish."

"No," I said, "feeling withdrawn is one thing I can really understand."

* * *

I missed my cat. So did Jake. He whined a lot and stared at me. I had posted signs, walked around the neighborhood, talked to merchants. Nobody knew anything.

I had all but given up hope.

I sat down on my bed, dangling my feet, trying to feel like a child.

I looked into the scarred mirror by the bed. The man in the mirror didn't have this infestation of memories. He was light as air. What was that old TV show I had seen as a kid, where a wife rushes into the attic just in time to see her husband's feet disappear into an old mirror? Something had dragged him inside and he never came out.

I thought about it. Horrible for the wife, maybe, but what of the man's fate? I couldn't decide.

"Maybe we'll get another cat, Jake," I said finally. I had a thick feeling in my chest. Jake was snoring, looked up, then fell back to sleep.

I shivered and pulled the comforter around my throat.

Day and night the din continued unabated. I bought earplugs for sleep. I made a cassette of soft music and played it all the time; lucky my tape deck had auto-reverse.

The phone rang one evening about eleven. I hated late phone calls, always picturing accidental death, fluorescent emergency rooms.

I calmed myself as I walked to the phone.

"Hello, Mr. West? This is Mrs. Ferguson. Your upstairs neighbor." I waited. So this creature of thunder and rage knew my name. "Your music—not that it's really that loud—but the letter of the law says eleven o'clock for noise—you did know that didn't you?—and I follow the letter of the law."

Blinds drawn all day, sleeping off the drugs, tell me about the law.

"Oh . . ." I said instead, my heart jumping into my throat, along with the words I was holding back, ". . . sorry. It's really soft, I'm surprised you can hear it." I had forgotten the music was on. I imagined her lying with her ears pressed to the floor, waiting for something to disturb her narcotic stupor.

"You know, the walls are thin, thin as paper. It wouldn't be so bad if I couldn't hear everything you do. When you go to the bathroom, when you eat, when you talk on the phone. And when you take a bath—your tub must be off-balance, it's like thunder when you take a bath."

"Oh, yeah, the landlord tried to fix that. The girl who lived here before—"

"Her," Mrs. Ferguson said. "She threw whiskey bottles. Out the window. In the middle of the night. I guess with everybody, it's something."

"Well, I guess it is," I said, growing impatient. "I hope that we can make the best of this . . . marriage." I hoped I sounded reasonable. "We're neighbors and we're going to have to compromise."

She didn't seem to hear me. "Sometimes during the day I have to go out, it gets so loud. The kids in the alley, your music . . ."

"Well, Mrs. Ferguson, I can hear you too," I said. She sucked in her breath as though I had punched her in the stomach.

"Well, when you live *over* someone, it's hard for them not to hear you. But noise coming up from underneath— it's like a bad dream."

You've been in your tower a little too long, princess, I wanted to say.

"We'll have to talk again," I said. "I have to go to bed now, I've got to get up early."

"I'm so glad we had this talk. I feel better already. I teach piano, you know, at home." I had never heard a piano, but didn't say so. I wondered how they made a living; you don't get paid to sleep.

At five A.M. the happy couple woke, threw a piece of furniture across the room, as if greeting the sun struggling

up through the hazy Oakland hills; I imagined them struggling on the floor for that last bit of white powder that
would bring down the cone of silence the rising sun had
threatened to destroy.

"**S**o what did you think of my boss?" I hadn't seen Janette since our encounter out front. We stood over the garbage cans as she shoved in an open bag and left off the lid. I held my neatly tied bag until my wrists began to ache, then laid it silently on the oil-stained concrete.

"Kinda ugly, a little too macho." Her face was turned away from the light, so I couldn't see her expression. "Am I being too brutal?"

"Brutal? You?" she asked, stretching the words. I wondered what she meant. "Fred is a little macho, I'll give you that, but he's got a great body." She turned around to face me.

Her eyes were blank for a moment; then they twinkled mischievously. She put a hand lightly on my shoulder. "Promise you won't tell anyone ..." She did not wait for the promise. "But I gave Fred a blow-job in the outer office the first day of work, after everyone had left."

She laughed, turning red. "Don't look at me like that. It just happened."

I laughed; the laugh spread, and shook me; I sat down on the garbage, trying to contain myself.

"I think he likes you," she continued after I had quieted down. "He couldn't stop talking about you all evening, even when—especially when—we were making love."

"My God," I said, "I thought he was giving me the male-dog look—stay away from my woman. You mean he wanted sex from me? I thought he wanted to kill me."

"He looks at you the same way he looks at me," she said. "This is San Francisco. I don't know why I fuck him, really. A mild amusement, giving him what he thinks he wants, what he thinks I am." She reached into her purse, white leather with a gold strap, slung over her shoulder. She pulled out a picture and handed it to me. She looked really pleased with herself. The picture was of a lovely dark-haired woman in an evening dress, delicate features, soft seductive eyes. "That's Margaret, my girlfriend."

"Your girlfriend?" I said. I said it twice, trying to make it sound real.

"Don't tell me you're shocked. Honestly, you Americans have the strangest double standards." Nonplussed, she moved into the alleyway, which was lit by a bare bulb. Behind her, her shadow was sharp and dark, large body, small head.

"I am not shocked," I said, trying to sound adult, and failing.

"Oh, yes you are," Janette said. "But you'll get over it. Think what a wonderful secret it is. No one knows about the two sides of me but you and Margaret." She opened the slatted front door, which cut out ribbons of twilight sky. "And of course myself."

Dumbfounded, I kept quiet.

"Oh, by the way, I heard the Fergusons talking this morning, out by the pool. They're moving, or at least looking. Soon you'll be home-free."

A couple Saturdays later, the Fergusons moved while I was at Safeway. A never-ending pain had suddenly relocated.

I set my groceries down, walked up the stairs. The door was open. The empty apartment looked surprisingly benign, sunlight pouring in, the view of the Bay (which I did not have) making the place seem larger than it was.

I walked downstairs slowly, worrying about melting ice cream, and listened. Nothing. It was as though a bell jar had descended. I picked up the groceries and took them inside. After I'd put things away, I put on some soft music, then turned it up. No response. I flushed my toilet, stood fully clothed in my noisy bathtub, and rocked.

No one heard. No one responded. I was free.

I enjoyed my exhilaration through the afternoon.

It clouded over and rain blew against the windows. There were flaws in the glass, like transparent roses.

I looked down at the swimming pool. The landlord had filled it last week. It was winter, no one would use it until spring, but I was glad.

I stood by the pool that night and watched the rain patter, circles crashing and breaking; thinking about all the freedom I was about to inherit, feeling tall and good and optimistic about the future.

When I looked at myself in the dark blue pool, I liked what I saw—a healthy man, proud swell of chest, my face the color of optimism.

I considered asking the landlord if I could move upstairs. I felt, somehow, that I could occupy the space in proper fashion. I was nursing a drink and thinking about picking up the phone. It was getting late, and did I really want to move again so soon?

I'd sleep on it.

Later that night, my fourth night of silence, a cold front swept down from the arctic and met tropical winds driving an armada of black clouds north.

At two A.M. the sky exploded. Lightning flickered like bombs on the horizon. The windows rattled, the electric lights sizzled and died.

The sky was a veined animal turned inside out.

Lightning cut across the housetops, disappeared into the horizon. In seconds the thunderclap hit, hard as a fist. It went on for hours.

I sat on my couch and watched, felt the windows shake, watched my image rattle as though the glass were now turned into wind-stirred water, my face coming clear in moments of stillness, then shivering and threatening to come apart as concussions of sound hit.

Across the way, through dripping leaves, I could see the rapt faces of other apartment dwellers, watching, waiting.

I smiled, imagining that they were waiting for lightning to strike, to fill them with the appearance of life.

With the will to move.

It was a nice day, a little warmer than it should have been. I was sitting by the pool.

Janette opened the hall window and leaned out. She had a blue towel wrapped around her head like a turban. "The landlord just stopped by to fix my sink," she called down. "He's rented the apartment above yours. You have a new neighbor. A decent guy, apparently. Very professional." She stopped, fixing the towel, which threatened to fall. "Oh, relax. My dear, you have a terrible time with trust, don't you? I can see that worried look even from here.

Frank (Apartment 3B, divorced with son) burst through the side door. He was wearing his jogging outfit. Janette fell silent, though she didn't close her window.

"Hello," he said, smiling wanly, then falling to the ground, where he pumped out a hundred perfect push-ups. The muscles of his back stood out like bricks. He got up, wiping his rough but not unhandsome features with his T-shirt. He had a small tattoo on his right upper arm, a serpent you had to look hard to see.

"Heard the news?" He looked at the open window and smiled. "The place is rented. The demons are out—I hear the new guy is a doctor, a regular joe."

There apparently was some sort of news network in the building that I was not privy to.

"How'd you find out?" I asked, trying to sound friendly

and unthreatened—I was a little embarrassed that the others in the building knew my problem. But maybe it was their problem too.

"Honestly, don't remember," Frank said. "Here's hoping that you'll be more lucky the second time around." Frank smiled. He grabbed my hand and pressed it, almost unwilling to let go.

I could hear Janette scurrying about in her window.

In a couple minutes there were heavy footsteps from the stairwell. We turned and waited.

Janette burst through the side door and left it flapping in the wind like a broken limb. Her hair was dripping from the shower. She toweled it while she walked, with exaggerated sensuality, swiveling her hips under a black silk robe.

"Boys, boys," she cried as she ran up, hugging us together. "What's up?"

Some of Frank's sweat stayed on my arm.

Frank looked embarrassed, fell out of the circle of arms, put on his stained shirt, then sat down on the edge of the pool.

"Have you seen him yet? Is he human?" I asked. I wondered suddenly if Janette had slept with Frank. Did everyone get initiated? And what was in store for the new tenant?

"No, but I saw him walking out with the landlord—broad back, tall—must have been six-foot-two, walked like he had something . . . well, you know, something to *give.*"

My question was answered.

I sat down next to Frank. Janette looked at us quizzically. Developing male friendships often puzzled women, made them feel left out. I had encountered the problem with Dorothy. The discomfort could lead to a rift in the friendship or the marriage.

I gestured for Janette to sit beside us, hoping to placate her cloudy fears.

Before long she had taken over the conversation. Frank grew so quiet I couldn't even hear his breath.

"When I was twelve, I used to summer on the Thames . . ." Janette said. She smiled, fingering her jade bracelet. She described how she and her uncle had wrestled in front of a roaring fire—while her aunt watched. She told the story slowly, relishing every detail.

"He couldn't keep his hands off me. I think he fancied me. My aunt never liked me much," she said, raising her long leathery fingers in a gesture of incomprehension. "I wonder why."

"Kids never know the effect they have on adults. They just know what gets attention," I said.

She turned to Frank. "Frank, our new neighbor, Michael, is so easy to talk to. Why, I've told him things already that I've never told anybody else."

"Excuse me," I said after a time. I was getting antsy. Janette seemed to have an endless array of amusing anecdotes. "I just remembered I've got some business upstairs."

I hobbled to the door that led to the alleyway—my feet had gone to sleep. I half-listened to Frank and Janette, to see if they thought I had left too abruptly. I am often the victim of impulses. The cries of blue jays in the giant palm tree, the soft movement of water in the pool, blurred the words.

I grabbed the doorknob. The door wouldn't budge. There was a brief tug-of-war.

Someone was coming out as I was going in.

I smiled and let go.

"Hello," he said as the door swung open. He remained in shadow and seemed a little larger than life. I remained myself to increase my gym regimen. "I heard voices and thought I'd introduce myself."

"Oh . . . hello," I said. "I'm . . . Michael West. I live . . ." I said, pointing, ". . . there."

"Paul Marks," he said. I couldn't see his face. I was looking into the dark, toward the stairs.

"Sorry, I've got to run," I said, feeling a diffuse nervousness. I looked at my left wrist, but wasn't wearing a watch. I shook his hand quickly. "I forgot an appointment. I'm sure we'll have plenty of time to talk later."

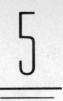

5

The phone rang that night at one o'clock. I answered it, by reflex, still dreaming.

An unnatural voice, like a bad actor auditioning for a part as a grave-robber, said, "Hello, a demon told me to have sex with you, *Michael West.*" In dreams, nothing is decisive; I could not conceive of anything as easy as putting the receiver down and going back to bed.

So I listened, dumbly. The thing on the other end of the line laughed hoarsely. Some sort of disease. The first coherent thought I had was that it was a friend playing a joke on me.

"That's interesting," I said, patiently waiting for the unveiling.

It continued undaunted. "Meet me in front of the museum tomorrow at three o'clock. I want to lick the smegma from your foreskin." (How did it know I was uncircumcised?)

There was more of the same, for about thirty seconds. Boring stuff, heard a thousand times before, from a thousand tired voices. I was waking up.

"What I think," I said in my best flat voice, "is that you've been taking the wrong drugs."

"The demon, the demon, the demon, told me to . . ." He screamed. (I had now determined its gender; women don't get off on this kind of provocation.)

Finally I hung up.

"Impotent prick," I said, trying not to be afraid, and climbed into bed.

Maniacs like that count on fear.

I slept fitfully. I woke with an erection at three A.M., that ominous time of most frequent deaths and births. At the sight of my unclothed body, blue-black and silver in the night-light, I began to masturbate.

In the mirror, the other Michael seemed to be having a good time. I watched him watching me. My pleasure grew exponentially. The tension crested, I pushed my hips in the direction of that silver surface, and something jumped through the air between us.

Then fell out of sight, swallowed by the dark separating him from me.

I lay back, enjoying the sticky warmth on my groin. My eyelids fluttered heavily, then shut, as waves of sleep crashed from below, and pulled.

There is a storm at sea, I thought. The waves are high, rising from the cold black ocean, crashing as white breakers which leave a foaming line on the sand.

I forced my eyes open for a second, to say good night to my counterpart.

As I sank into sleep, the man in the mirror stood up.

The next day was Saturday. I had no plans, except to relax. I can never relax when I plan to.

There were some new noises coming from upstairs. I tried to shut them out. I didn't want to establish a troublesome relationship from the start. But, boy, I thought, sitting on the arm of a chair, he sure didn't waste any time moving in.

Though he couldn't be half as bad as the Fergusons— there was only one of him.

I crawled back into bed. I watched a *Lucy* rerun. I read the morning paper.

I tried but couldn't go back to sleep.

The sun was full up, rising behind the blinds, heating

the room. Sweat had made my bed a puddle. I put the sheets between my clenched legs to absorb the moisture. I tried counting sheep (first time ever), but they came out distorted—like knots of muscle without skin, ceaselessly jumping over a fence, and then back again.

I tried to imagine the sound of running water (this also helps me urinate), but I kept seeing the pool in the back-yard, still, blue, with black leaves floating on the surface.

I wasn't sleepy, but I wanted to waste time. It was my time to waste. It was Saturday. Finally I got up and opened the blinds. The pale sun moved into a vaporous yellow-blue sky. I made some coffee, and the smell gave me some hope.

I burned my tongue on the boiling coffee.

I read the entertainment section at the kitchen table, and drank more coffee, now tepid; amazing how fast heat gets lost.

Smell of bacon and eggs, laughter, windows opening, an argument through one of those open windows. Dull, com-forting sounds. The building was waking up too.

I tried to distinguish my new neighbor's contribution to the symphony, but could not. He must be awfully orga-nized. I remembered the agonizing days it had taken me to get my furniture arranged.

Before I knew it, the morning was gone.

Outside, the sky was sulfurous, the breeze faintly oily.

I passed a couple whose faces were already familiar—a frumpy man in ill-fitting clothes, and his female compan-ion, also frumpy, long hair cut short on top only and dyed green. Since they were together, they didn't say hello; the woman was quite friendly when she was alone.

I warmed up, and started jogging. Jake ran circles around me, barking and trying to trip me. He was eight years old and a little retarded. Sweet, but his brain con-stantly misfired. One blue eye, one brown.

I had had him fixed a couple of years before, because he got into fights. I found that if I climbed up on something when another male dog approached, then a fight could be avoided. But I couldn't always find higher ground.

I wondered if somewhere in his mind he didn't bear the slightest resentment for what I had done to him.

A second shower, a long basking in front of the mirror, watching the sun play on flushed muscles.

I opened the window; the breeze was chilly. The fog had started to come in; there was an unprecedented heat wave in the central valley—a hundred and ten every day, as hot as Death Valley—and the inner heat drew the fog into the Bay.

Patricia sat by the pool, dressed in a red-and-gray wool coat and dangling bare feet in the water.

She looked truly innocent; not "the new innocence" but the real unconscious kind.

I threw on a fresh sweatshirt and pants and went down the back stairs.

"Hi," I said. "I thought I'd join you. It's a little chilly, but welcome to summer in the Bay." She smiled. I took off my shoes and sloshed water with my big ugly feet. Patricia's feet were small and translucent; I kept thinking of the bound feet of Oriental princesses.

She put a slender long-fingered hand on my arm; friendly and without guile.

"Didn't I see you once in a Macy's ad?" I asked. My feet were turning blue.

"Oh, once, a year ago or so. They paid me peanuts, and drove me crazy. I don't like modeling—they treat you like . . . a doll." She said the last word venomously; I pulled my feet from the water.

"I used to rip the eyes out of my dolls when I was a kid," she said, laughing. "So I guess everything comes full circle."

"I don't know," I said. I wasn't sure what she meant, but it sounded good.

"How about you?" Patricia asked. "You said you worked in a hospital or something."

"Yeah," I said, feeling very much the part of the lowly

clerk. "Sometimes you can't tell the patients from the employees." I worked in psychiatry. I wanted to make it sound romantic. It wasn't. "One therapist—who looks like a bag lady—spends fifteen minutes in the bathroom before she sees a patient. I would kill to know what she does in there."

Patricia laughed. "Maybe she's putting on a new face."

"But she always comes out with the same one," I laughed.

"Psychiatry," Patricia mused. "You must know something . . . about dreams."

Patricia ran upstairs and was back in flash. She clutched a tattered black notebook to her chest. "I write down interesting dreams," she said. "Want to hear one?"

Her eyes took on a faraway look. "There are two best friends," she read, "who witness an alien invasion. The girls are in an alley doing speed. They see something in the dark. It turns out to be an insectoid thing, half-roach and half-alligator. It walks like a man."

"Like the old song," I said, starting to laugh.

"The girls are so loaded," Patricia continued, "that they don't know if the insect thing is real or not. Whatever it is, it is looking for something. It finds it. Another creature like itself, which crawls out of a trashcan. The two creatures kiss, then take off, faster than any man can move."

Patricia looked perturbed. "Then the dream changes scene. The girls are sleeping on the floor in an empty apartment. One of them wakes up. She rolls over and sees an insect creature peeling the flesh from her friend's face. She gets up and leaves the room. In the street she sees several more of the creatures; people on the street don't seem to notice anything strange. She decides she might have power over the creatures, since only she can see them. She leads them to an apartment building she knows, where there are several people who have treated her badly. She climbs into a tree at the back of the building and watches the creatures climb up the side of the building, break the windows, and go inside. She hears them eating the tenants. When she climbs down, the creatures are everywhere; there aren't many people in the street. Some of the creatures are wearing the clothes of the people they have eaten. The creatures are screwing all over the place, multiplying. The baby aliens fall in the girl's hair. They are like roaches, but have human faces. They are survivors."

"That's an interesting dream," I said.

6

"**S**he sounds like a real nut case to me." Janette had lifted the hood of my car and was looking intently inside. "Try it again," she said.

A thick sound came from the engine, there was a brief stutter, then silence.

"Patricia is just sensitive, psychic. One of those people that everything funnels through. I am kind of worried about her, though—too vulnerable, you know. An easy target." My voice trembled, which I tried to control. I was thinking about the rapt expression on Patricia's face as she had told her goofy story, the flush on her cheeks.

Janette, wearing a pink silk blouse, had lowered herself to the asphalt and slid under the car.

"I saw Paul Marks this morning. So far he's the original invisible man." All I could see were her tanned ankles and lavender pumps. "Good-looking. A doctor, or you already know that, I bet. You've been initiated into the Information Society."

"Yes, I have," I said.

"I don't know that's wrong with the bloody thing," she said after a couple of minutes in her heaviest cockney accent. I smiled. "Do you need a lift somewhere?" she asked, standing up and brushing off her pants, which were unsoiled.

She walked to the center of the road. Behind her, our

apartment building looked like an empty shell. It was hard to believe anything lived there. Strange image, I thought; until just that moment I had thought the building looked ... well, homey.

"No, I don't need a ride," I shouted over the roar of her car, which she had climbed into and started—the top was down. "I thought I'd stick around here and feel things out." She smiled brightly. She had been going to the sun-tanning parlor three times a week, heightening the contrast.

"And you should put up the top at night. You're entirely too trusting. This isn't England, you know. And winter's coming on. It could rain," I said, but I doubted that she heard.

Giving me a quick glance in her rearview mirror, she was off in a spray of cinders and dust.

I ran into Frank on my way back into the lobby.

"Car's on the blink," I said disconsolately, my eyes slowly getting used to the dark. Someone stood behind him, whom I first mistook for a shadow, though the angle of the sun argued against it.

Startled, I took a step backward.

"This is my son, Brian," Frank said, pulling the boy from behind him. "Brian comes to visit most weekends, but he's been busy lately, field trips to the Sierras and stuff." Frank's voice had a slight edge of discomfort.

I took the boy's cool small hand and shook it. "Nice to meet you, Brian," I said. "What grade are you in?" I never knew what to say to children, although they usually seemed to like me.

"Second," he said firmly. The boy was pale, fleshy, round-eyed, unhealthy-looking; you could see the veins through his powdery flesh, thin blue lines like pencil markings. Hard to imagine him as Frank's son.

By the stubborn turn of his head as he stared intently at his feet, I knew that further conversation was useless.

Soon he moved off to a stained-glass window that looked

into the side alley while Frank and I made small talk. The weather, mostly. Were we in for another drought? What was a thermal inversion . . . would you like to be a weatherman with this crazy weather? That sort of thing.

I watched Brian from the corner of my eye; Frank had turned his back to him. The boy had found a tiny break in the leaded glass and worked his finger through.

I started to say something, but stopped myself.

Instead, I walked around Frank so he was forced to look in Brian's direction if he wanted to look at me.

"Resembles his mother?" I asked, circling. Frank nodded tiredly, his eyes fixed on an invisible point in the middle of the air.

Brian made a sharp clucking sound, like a cat that had seen a bird.

"Careful, Brian," Frank said, although Brian's back now hid what he was doing with his hands. I could see the mantle of fatherhood squatting on Frank's shoulders like a demon.

Brian pulled back quickly at his father's voice.

He walked toward us with a curiously blank expression on his face, a bubble of blood on his cut finger.

He stared at it as though it were unreal, the blood coming from somebody else.

"Here, let me see," Frank said, his voice soft yet irritated.

"Nah," Brian said, pulling back and sucking the cut. "Doesn't hurt."

"Wrap it in this anyway," Frank said, handing the red-lipped boy a black handkerchief.

"So where are you off to?" I asked. "Nice day, no rain yet, though I think another storm would . . . cleanse things."

"To the zoo; Brian loves the zoo." Frank looked pained. Brian walked out the front door. The lobby smelled ancient, from the musty old carpet, and strangely new, from the Velcro-like stuff the landlord had put on the stairs, which smelled like glue; the breeze stirred things up a bit, but the two opposing elements, like oil and water, would not mix.

"You have my sympathy," I said. Frank grabbed my shoulder. His eyes lingered on mine, as though he wished I could rescue him, but I felt a little embarrassed and pulled away.

"Animals in cages, big concrete cages," Frank said as he left. "I'll never get used to it. But Brian—Brian can't get enough of it."

As the door closed and I was alone, someone came out of an apartment upstairs. A slight vibration like a passing truck, that grew stronger. The footsteps were heavy, but the descent was quick.

I made a dash for the second floor—having had my quota of social intercourse that day—and had barely gotten the key in the lock when he was on me.

I turned the key, but I had inadvertently tried the side-door key. No movement.

I had no choice but to withdraw the key and turn around to face him. You have to live with people, so you don't do what you really feel.

He was big, a full head taller than I was. He held out his hand. Blinding white smile, perfect teeth, wide shoulders. He stood as erect as any man I had ever seen.

I wondered if he rehearsed his posture in front of the mirror for hours each day. Nothing else could explain it.

"Sorry I couldn't stay and talk the other day," came the perfectly modulated voice. Huh? I thought I was the one who left. "I thought I heard the phone."

Heard the phone from two stories down, with the windows closed? Inhuman ears.

What kind of story was this? I was tempted to ask, but again repressed myself. My astigmatic eyes couldn't focus when things were too close. He was a double blur, which seemed to spread.

"Oh, that's fine, fine," I said, feeling like I wanted to hurry off somewhere, get away from the weird feeling that had crept up on me. "Moving is a big hassle—I know, I just moved in a few weeks ago myself. Scatters you into a million pieces. Takes time to put the puzzle back together."

He moved his large square head with its flat ears and jutting jawline—chin cleft, unshaved, apparently so that it would appear deeper—in a way that in a dog would have meant puzzlement. He stared at me blankly. Were his eyes gray or brown?

"If there's any problem, be sure to let me know," he said, starting to walk down the stairs. His arms were perfect half-circles. The words fell to the floor and burst with a hollow popping sound. Extensive history of cocktail parties; habits insincere and disdainful; underestimates everyone. Used to success and getting his way.

He continued, staring a hole through me from the bottom of the stairs. "Noises, stomping around, whatever. Don't be . . . shy."

Was it growing darker inside? I would have to talk to the landlord about having the inside lights turned on during the day.

For a brief moment I felt something inside my head snap, like a bone breaking. I was sure I had just blown an aneurysm; that would account for the slow darkening. I grabbed the doorknob for support, against a sudden spinning sensation and a downward pull as though someone had opened a door on vacuum.

Patricia's dream came back to me in vivid detail; and I swear as my upstairs neighbor moved, I could easily see, with only a little imaginative effort, one of those flesh-eating insects walking through the lobby, instead of a man.

"By the way," he/it said from the base of the stairs, not noticing that I was flying apart. I fumbled through my keys, finally found the right one.

"My name is Dr. Paul Marks. Plastic surgeon. Here's my

card," he said, and left it on the windowsill by the front door.

I nodded dumbly and opened my door. I barely made it inside to the haven of my mirror.

I sat up late into the night. The air was dead and still.
Jake was asleep at the foot of the bed, his feet sticking
into the air like those of an embalmed animal.

The wind shivered the windowpanes in their loose
frames. No explosions, nothing dramatic; just wind and old
putty.

I had been filled with a vague dread since my encounter
in the hallway with my new neighbor. Nothing tangible, just
a feeling that something wasn't right—a premonition. We
had scarcely exchanged a dozen words—so what was the
problem?

After an hour of circular thinking, I came to the conclusion that it was jealousy. He was upstairs, I was down: we
were dogs. He had found the higher ground I secretly
longed for.

I likened the feeling, after a few more minutes of dry
rumination, to falling in love with a woman you don't know.
Sudden and overpowering, like drowning. Something you
can't explain, and maybe don't want.

Uncontrollable and sourceless, you are at its mercy.

Fear and love: twined together, warriors bound up to
the death. They felt the same in my chest, crashing and
consuming. It was like being on a road and suddenly finding that you had taken a wrong turn and ended up in a
swamp. The road you followed was no road at all.

I thought of Janette, as an excuse to get away from the

cloying thoughts about my new upstairs neighbor. Maybe I could translate laterally.

I tried to imagine being in love with Janette. We had had sex; we had had something. I should have some feelings. But I couldn't find any. Dependence, obsession—those were possible. Fear of her attention straying, of another man entering my territory.

I sat and stared a hole in the ceiling. When would Janette initiate Paul Marks officially into the building? I think she was out tonight. Was she with him?

I got up and paced. Two o'clock, three o'clock; I watched Jake.

I thought about Dorothy—when nothing is happening, think about the past. She had walked out on Christmas Eve. I guess she had been right to go. I hadn't provided her much happiness. Over time, she had begun to wither under my touch.

I went to the mirror and asked a question.

"Michael," I whispered, face to silver surface, "Michael, what is going on?"

The face in the mirror looked healthy, unlined, vigorous, quite different from how I felt. Perhaps the pacing had given me—had given him—an aerobic edge.

I ran fingers through my hair, which seemed thicker and darker than usual. I have mood hair.

I brushed my teeth, pulled on striped pajama bottoms, and climbed between the cool sheets.

I masturbated three times before I finally got to sleep.

I was shaving. I pulled the straight razor over a two-day growth of beard, and memories sprang into my head as little beads of blood appeared.

My father had been an ardent hunter. Every year he took me to a hunting lodge the week after Thanksgiving; the lodge was a hundred miles north. The forest in that blue northern region was thick with deer.

I remembered the heavy snow, trampled from the boots

of hunters. The way the black, wet boughs hung down and slapped my face as I followed my father, a rifle in his hand.

He would motion me into stillness with a backward movement of a gloved hand, and I would freeze until the shot rang out.

Then I rushed forward with him, as if pulled by an invisible string, to see what we had killed.

One day he had shot a doe by accident. Her fawn was wandering aimlessly about, occasionally nuzzling the bleeding carcass. The snow was covered with blood, as though someone had tossed rose petals.

Father shot the fawn.

"Wouldn't live long anyway," he had said, no feeling in his voice.

Behind a dark mantle of tangled bare branches I saw the antlers of the buck as he turned away slowly, fading back into the trees.

Father raised the rifle again and fired.

"You're what I'm after," Father shouted as the deer fell in a lazy arc, headfirst, then the powerful hind legs twitching, kicking the snow in a final spasm.

Father jumped over the doe and fawn, running to his prize. I followed, more slowly this time, stepping carefully over the spilled blood.

I shook my head to clear it of the memory, then finished shaving.

When I washed off the green shaving cream, I exposed a whitish gash. I looked for the styptic pencil.

Strangely, although the cut was deep and the flesh furrowed, it did not bleed.

The cut began to bleed as I walked into the hall.

Janette was coming stealthily down the stairs, holding on to the wall as though she were about to faint. She looked pale and drawn, and her eyes had the vacant stare of an autistic child's.

We were almost face-to-face before she acknowledged me.

"Oh, God, Michael—it's you." She looked embarrassed.

She stared at the gray-brown rug, as though trying to focus her eyes, then shook her head. "Boy, do I feel weird this morning. Like I got Alzheimer's disease overnight." Then she looked up. "Michael, you're bleeding all over the place." She touched my face helplessly, withdrawing a reddened finger.

The blood was warm, not unpleasant, trickling down my neck. "Cut myself while shaving," I said.

"Here, let's go inside," she said, taking my arm and leading me back into my apartment.

"What were you doing upstairs?" I asked.

"Oh, visiting—the new man," she said, attempting a smile. "Don't look at me like that. I am a hopeless romantic."

"I thought I heard your voice late last night," I said. "I thought maybe I was dreaming."

"Oh, this building's walls are thin as paper," she said, pressing a towel against the cut.

When the wound had clotted and Janette had gone home, still looking sheepish and saying nothing specific about her night with Paul Marks, I felt dry and lonely, and wished the blood would start to flow again.

The building whispered at night.

There were words being spoken, just below the level of hearing. It was hard to distinguish between the roar of a car, the distant cries of fighting cats, the pulse of music, and voices speaking.

I was taking too many sleeping pills. Could that account for the fog of sounds? I lay in bed watching the ceiling, listening, waiting for something to disturb me.

It took me a good hour to get going in the morning, and a full pot of coffee to rip away the veil my dreamless sleep had left: scum on a pond. I was late to work twice—completely out of the ordinary for me.

My boss thought it was a woman. I could tell when she passed by, that look of all-knowing sympathy. I felt like telling her that she was half-right, that it was part woman, part howling void colliding inside me.

Barbara questioned me gently one day. She knew better than to confront me directly. I had always kept my private life private from her. Even during the divorce, I had shared little of my pain with her, perhaps because she was my supervisor and it didn't seem appropriate.

Also, I had an image of myself—of quiet reserve and strength—that I wanted to maintain in her eyes.

"Michael," Barbara said, coming up behind me. Her voice seemed far away; I was wearing a headset and listening to a droning neurologist detailing one of his notoriously malingering patients. "Michael, you look a little tired lately. Are you well?"

Barbara was short, Jewish, black hair shot with gray. She had had two husbands, the first who died of a coronary, the second an invalid for the last two years of their marriage, whom she nursed until his death six months ago. Rumor had it that she was seeing another man, older, and also not well. I wondered, briefly, what she got out of putting herself through her lovers' deaths—as I framed a careful answer to her question.

"Oh, sorry, didn't hear." I pulled off the headset slowly, buying more time. My thoughts were sluggish. "Did you say I wasn't looking well? I'm insulted. You know how vain I am."

"No, Michael, you always look fine, even when you're not. But you seem ... exhausted, drained. Like your thoughts are somewhere else. Maybe it's time you took that vacation to Mexico. A week on the beach would do you a world of good." She laughed. "Maybe I'll come with you."

"I can't go just yet. I like to stick close to home on the holidays. And my new apartment is just coming together, getting comfortable."

We chatted some more, office politics, a birthday party for someone. She probed a bit more, but gave up when I wouldn't open up. Her words, though well-intended, were like raindrops beading on a raincoat.

As she turned to leave she asked, "Michael, are you dyeing your hair? There are dark hairs all through the blond now. I couldn't help but notice; that light is right over your head. Or maybe my old eyes just aren't seeing clearly."

"Hormonal changes," I said, keeping my voice light and airy. I wanted to charge to the nearest mirror. "Men go through those too, although they're not as ... well, dramatic as the changes women go through."

"Michael, if you need anything, let me know," she said a little peevishly, and closed the door.

* * *

There was a small balcony outside my bedroom window and a planter box over the front rim, which I intended to fill with flowers when I had the time. A potted palm had been left by the former tenant (the dancer/whiskey drinker). I meant to throw the half-eaten palm out, but hadn't gotten around to it. I suspected cats were crawling up the pipes when I was out, and feasting.

I missed my cat. Cats are sneaky and unpredictable. Dogs rarely surprise you.

I didn't have any plans for the evening. I found myself walking from mirror to mirror, glaring.

Making faces in the bathroom, watching myself in the glass over the Miró print (and not seeing the print at all), in the closet mirror, the shard of mirror I use for looking at the back of my hair, etc.

I vaguely considered breaking the mirrors to see what, if anything, would be released. But I couldn't risk the bad luck—seven times seven: all the time I had left (if I were lucky).

Instead, I pounded the shiny tabletop where darkening Michael stared up, startled by the overly emotional face, features distorted by hidden, half-understood feelings. My face shimmered like an image in a lake stirred by wind.

I could go out for a walk, but the evening was chilly and dry. There was no wind and the air was as still as death; there was a sea out there, somewhere, but you'd never have known it.

I considered driving to the ocean, to make sure it hadn't disappeared. My first years here I went to the ocean a lot, even on foggy days, especially on foggy days, because the cliffs were deserted. The fog was like smoke from a burning sea. I could think undisturbed about the endless curl of waves from here to there. Hagfish in the coldest depths, burrowing into their prey; the rush of fish in the coral reefs, beautiful brief colors in shallow warm waters, then the plunge into the icy depths, where darker, colder things moved.

As I was just about to get my coat, I heard footsteps in

the hall, went to the door, and peered around the heavy paper blind. It was Janette, wearing pink and blue.

I needed to hear another voice, a sort of grounding for the undirected surge of my imagination and loneliness.

"Hello, Janette." I had opened the door. My voice was a little shaky. "Off somewhere? Have time to come in for some brandy? Korbel? Your favorite."

She looked tired, smiled, then came in. She was silent, looked at me rather blankly. Her eyes flashed a couple of times, dimly, like a TV screen before it blows, and there was a rictus about her mouth instead of her usual sensual pout.

I poured two brandies while she sat by the window, looking out, paying me no mind. She drank the brandy slowly, put it down carefully on the table, not taking her eyes from the yard below.

"Damned hard to see," she said finally, flatly. "You should get the landlord to cut back that tree. Almost totally blocks your view."

I made small talk, counted the ticking of the clock, waiting for the brandy to release the Janette I knew. When she finished the drink, I offered her another, which she refused.

A footstep overhead, sharp, decisive, well-defined. Janette started, as though struck. Her expression was confused and ugly, like cars colliding. She got up slowly, with deliberate restraint.

"Got to go now," she said, giving my shoulder a cursory pat. "There's something I have to tell Paul."

Before I could stop her, she was out the door and up the stairs.

I sat down, listening to the patterns of footsteps on the ceiling, from kitchen to living room, then one pair into the bedroom. I was an expert on identifying footsteps; everyone in the building was now in my catalog. Janette's voice rose, I could hear her almost as clearly as if she stood before me; there was no reply for the longest time. I waited with bated breath.

Then it came, a loud hollow laugh that seemed to shake the walls, like the concussion of an earth tremor. There was a scuffling then, a slamming of the front door. Janette shot past my door, into the lobby, and into the street.

I heard her car start, the squeal as she held the key turned too long, then the roar of the engine and screeching tires. I had walked into the hall. The building was a wind tunnel of sound.

I looked down the stairway. Janette's feelings lingered in the air, a series of snapshots of herself descending the stairs, eyes red, hands feeling the dark in front of her streaming eyes, shoulders hunched forward protectively like a child defending itself from its parents.

I had no way of really knowing, but it seemed right.

Aftermath of a one-nighter. Apparently Janette and Paul Marks did not see their relationship the same way.

From overhead came a new sound. A dry insistent squall, like that of a tyrannical child who had gotten his way but was still not satisfied.

9

"**P**lastic surgery," he said, "control your own destiny."

I laughed faintly, cringing inside. That black wave of anxiety was sweeping up from somewhere. I couldn't let it show. This man, who held his face straight up so that nothing could leak out, was not one to show weakness before. My gut feeling was strong.

"Dr. Marks," I started.

"Paul, please call me Paul," he said sincerely. I was tempted to believe, but remained suspicious. "I get so tired of titles at the hospital."

"Okay, Paul. How'd you get into that line?" I looked at his face briefly, features overly large, expansive cheekbones, flat ridge down his generous nose, as though a sculptor's blade had moved down it. A product of another surgeon's fantasy, or his own, directing another's hand? How much was genuine?

"Oh, when I went to college, I didn't have any particular interests. Premed seemed the way to go, and then I ran into an older woman—or she ran into me—who had had a deformed face as a child. A beautiful woman now, perfect. She was as beautiful and remote as any woman I had ever met, as though she had been beautiful all her life. I saw pictures of her as a child. Horrible. I could never forget it. When I looked at her I saw two things. I got involved with her anyway—naive buck, you know—and she dumped me when it got too serious. So I had my vocation chosen for me—by love, as it were. Maybe to recreate her." He paused, holding a fleshy long-fingered hand to a cleft chin. "Or maybe it was the money. I never liked being poor. General practitioners don't make dirt. A dying breed."

I wondered what Janette would look like when I saw her next.

"Why, if you don't mind me asking, are you living in this building? This isn't the highest rent district. I'd see you as being more a Pac Heights man."

"No," he said, his eyes bright as aluminum, "I wanted something small, something intimate. It's a need I often have—to get away from things. When I saw the place, I knew this was about as far away as I could get." He laughed rather unpleasantly, then swallowed the laugh, as though he had given something away.

"Michael," Patricia said gently, then more firmly, "Michael, are you okay? You look like you've seen a ghost."

I laughed, looked at her finely boned face, pale as a china doll's, and said, "No, trying to avoid seeing one."

Patricia laughed heartily and her Adam's apple, a bone no larger than a child's knuckle, moved up and down with the musical sound.

"Oh, you mean . . . the new tenant. I wondered how long it would take you to get irritated. You are a sensitive soul, you know." She smirked; then her expression became more serious, as though a distasteful thought had crossed her mind.

"There's something strange about him. He's kind of there and not there at the same time. You know?"

"Yeah, I've noticed," Patricia said. "But most people seem like that now. A lot of them. Don't take it too seriously."

"It has more to do with Janette," I said. "I don't really know anything about this guy at all. I've only talked to him a couple of times. Bizarre, sort of—what's the word?—evocative. That's not right. But you know, sets all kinds of things loose in me.

He gives me the creeps, and he's involved with Janette some-how—"

"Janette, it's always Janette. She gets her fingers into everything."

"What do you mean—always?" I said, knowing the answer.

"She makes a habit of sleeping with the new men in the building, sort of like a dog peeing on a tree to mark its territory. In some ways, she is very masculine."

The blood continued to rush into my face until words were unnecessary.

"Oh, no, not you." Patricia gave me a brief, surprisingly strong hug, trying to hide her smile. "Well, of course you. You'd have been the only one she hasn't hit on who wasn't gay. And she's tried that too." A smile broke out on her face. "You've got to admit it's kind of funny."

"I wish I could laugh," I said, standing still under the embrace. "But my mind is confused right now. Maybe it's the move. Maybe it's the holidays or loneliness, or whatever. But I have this strange feeling—"

"Well, the holidays always throw me for a loop," Patricia said. "But soon they'll be over and then we have the new year."

"Janette is quite a character. I do have some affection for her, I guess," I said. "Last night I heard an argument between her and . . . Paul Marks that turned my stomach. I couldn't make out the words, but I got the feeling he was getting off on rejecting her. You know the type—gets more pleasure out of withholding than giving."

"Sure, anal personality type, mostly men. I wonder why that is? But I wouldn't worry too much about Janette. She's nobody's fool. She's been around the world several times. Let's just wait and see what happens." Patricia had started down the stairs. "I have to go now. I have a small part in a play."

I brightened. "I'd love to see you perform. Let me know when and where."

"If it's any good, I'll let you know. I don't think it's going to be much of a part—not like Juliet in the balcony scene. This is a fast suicide number—and she jumps to her death early on in the play. I must infuse it with meaning. I must get ready," she said in a pleasant self-effacing tone.

"I've got to get inside too," I said a little sharply.

"Off we go, then, to our separate fantasies. Until we meet again." She laughed and hurried out the door.

I put on a little soft music, I read the evening paper, scanned the TV listings. With forty-three channels you'd think there'd have been something to watch.

I made a quick dinner, stir-fried vegetables and fifteen-minute brown rice, and ate it in five minutes, in front of the evening news. It (the food; on the news I reserved judgment) was flavorless, but nourishing. I didn't feel better, though I knew I had done the right thing for my body.

The record ended, Vanna White was modeling a new gown, and I flipped the set off with my foot. Now I had to plan my evening, or risk staring at the walls and thinking—and I knew where that sort of contemplation would lead: from the mirror to the wall, to the ceiling, transformed thoughts pouring back into me like black water.

Sure enough, in fifteen minutes I was in deep water. Somewhere a baby was crying. There was a sudden percussion, the window glass shook, and I waited for the wave of earth that meant earthquake, jump under a table, or get out of the building if you think you have the time.

Then came the footsteps. A crowd of noisy footsteps, unfamiliar. The front door to the building opened again and again. The whole world seemed to be coming up the steps. I got lost trying to distinguish one from another. Coats scratched my front door, voices stopped and then suddenly moved upward.

For what seemed like hours I listened to the echo of the front-door buzzer, the pounding feet, always going up; I wondered that Paul's floor could hold the weight.

Oh, boy, a party, I thought. What fun. I lay there feeling the room shaking about me. The louder it got, the stiller I became. It seemed the ceiling bowed and would collapse. Strangers would rain down on me.

Allergies, I thought, getting up; trying to smash back the murderous fury that was rising through me. This is pure ear-canal stuff, change of pressure from histaminic reaction, nothing fanciful or threatening.

Calm down; people have a right to walk up the stairs without your permission.

There was the thunder of footsteps across the ceiling, increasing as the minutes passed, a tide of movement from kitchen to living room to bathroom. Were they playing tag? I suspected some chemical substances were being abused.

Muffled voices, shattering of a glass (or something), a window opening, then quickly closing.

I walked to my bedroom window (I imagined the coats lying on the bed in the room above, like the shed skins of snakes). I opened the window, testing the breeze. Cold, but dry, no hint of rain. Smell of dead fish, gasoline, and a faintly musty smell that I was not able to identify.

The pool glowed like phosphorescent pond water under a tepid half-moon. No one was sitting there: I had been half-hoping that Patricia had gone down for one of her late-evening meditations after her rehearsal. Another sensitive soul. We could moan together.

I vaguely considered going down alone, but I didn't want the people upstairs to see me.

Everyone had parties. Paul Marks was handsome, successful, had lots of friends; much networking would be required to maintain his life-style. It made sense.

I leaned out the window backward, holding the sill with my hands, hoping to catch the flicker of shadows on the drawn shades.

I teetered dangerously, almost lost my grip, and then pulled back inside.

In the bathroom I pretended to brush my teeth while really looking at my face.

Sharp teeth, increasingly angular jawline, looked too good to be true. I felt awful. The eyes that used to swim from emotion to emotion, from strength to weakness, eyes that had never remained steady, stared out at me like steel balls.

I turned off the light, ran my hands down my chest, untying my sweatpants and letting them drop to my ankles.

The downstairs door opened, and Janette's familiar patter up the stairs interrupted my masturbatory fantasy.

I leaned over carefully, exercising abdominal muscles, then stretching out vertebra by vertebra as I rose, pulling up my pants.

It was difficult to make out, but I thought that Janette passed by Paul Marks's door, entered her own apartment without closing her door, then rang Paul's bell.

At any rate, there was a rush to the front door upstairs, which I felt in my spine and in my feet.

A burst of voices, silenced by the closing door. So now Janette was inside, at the site of her earlier distress or humiliation.

I moved back to my bedroom. All sexual thoughts seemed to drain from me like stagnant water down an opening drain. I slipped on a T-shirt; the sight of my body was suddenly repulsive.

I opened the window again; before I knew it, I had crawled out onto the balcony, with my back to the railing, looking up to see what I could see.

The living-room windows were shrouded; and I could not see the bedroom windows because of the balcony above, somewhat larger than mine, which had planter boxes already rioting with flowers. A quick move-in, quick adjustment. I looked at my empty planter boxes and swallowed hard.

The noise reached a crescendo, remained steady, then lessened. An hour, an hour and a half. I was stiff as a board. I stayed out on the balcony. Apparently some of the gang were leaving. There were muffled good-byes. A window opened and this time was left open.

There were still a few voices wafting down to me on the

dry winter wind, and I caught scraps of conversation, which I managed to piece together.

This gathering was a housewarming of sorts, which was to continue later at Club Nouveau, a local nightclub with an infamous door policy.

Thank God, I thought; maybe I'll get some sleep tonight after all. (Unless, of course, they come home afterward and continue the party.)

Then I heard Janette's voice, soft and pleading, rising above the others.

Embarrassed and sickened, I wanted not to listen, but couldn't stop myself.

Paul Marks's strong footsteps carried him from the French doors that separated the bedroom from the living room, where the few remaining guests must have been.

"Excuse me," Paul Marks said, "I have some business to take care of—in here."

There was laughter, a cessation of movement in the living room.

The dark water sloshed about in my chest, like the weak waves of a storm's aftermath. I could hardly breathe. I looked beyond the balcony to the sky; there were no stars, only lights from the city illuminating a yellow haze.

Before I knew what I was doing, I had found a handhold and was pulling myself out onto the ledge. I found a solid railing and pulled myself up to the upper balcony with one swift silent movement.

The living-room windows were still shaded, so I didn't think that I would be detected from there (though I was hardly thinking at all, or I'd have been downstairs with earplugs in, and sleeping). And judging from the sounds emanating from the bedroom, I doubted that gunfire would have interrupted Janette and Paul from what they were doing.

There were opalescent curtains on the windows to the upper balcony, the kind of material cheap bridesmaids' dresses are made of. I could see the shape of the bed, and fuzzy white light everywhere. When Janette and Paul, who paced around each other like animals trying to figure out who was predator and who was prey, passed near the curtains, I saw pastel shadows, though it was hard to tell one from the other.

Finally there was a slap, sharp as a fired bullet, then a cry; more of Janette's pleading, and a hollow laugh— presumably Paul's. Then responding laughter from Janette, coy, high-pitched, halfhearted.

Paul ripped open the curtains, though he took no notice of me. He was looking over his shoulder across the way, at a distant row of windows.

He was naked, shoulders knotted, every muscle standing out, like scales; his buttocks were perfect half-globes, and when he moved, the muscles moved sinuously under shiny olive-colored flesh.

Janette knelt in front of the ornate brass bed, holding her face in her hands.

Paul looked at her, then away; his expression was one of mild distaste, as if the cuisine did not fit his taste. A woman at his feet. A mild inconvenience, at best.

He then turned dramatically to the window, flexing every muscle unnecessarily in the gesture. I lowered myself slowly, though he was looking out and away, toward the sky, not at me.

I almost lost my grip. He swaggered to the window. His huge limp penis swung like a pendulum. It was as large as an arm, veined, moist, and curving.

He pressed his naked body to the glass, making love to his own image.

Behind him, Janette cried. He pulled himself angrily from the glass, as if rudely wakened.

He pushed her onto the floor; her eyes were wet but blank. She looked up at his erection, which he slapped across her face.

Then he fell upon her. He moved furiously, as though performing in a sadistic pornographic film.

My arms ached. I didn't know how much longer I could

hold on. I'd lost feeling in my hands. I was frozen in horror and fascination.

I found a foothold on the side of the building, which took some of the weight from my hands. I looked at the French doors, which had parted slightly; the remaining partygoers were looking in, their eyes having that glassy imbecilic quality of people who watch TV too much.

Janette had moved to the bed. Paul rose on his knees like a horse about to trample someone, and his right hand moved furiously against his groin, pumping in and out.

He rose to his fullest height under the rhythmic insistence of his fingers.

And then with a single thrust he was inside her.

As I lowered myself, I saw his eyes, staring blankly at the wall, while his body moved, dutiful and passionless.

"**A**re you sure you weren't dreaming?" Patricia asked, her eyes as round as saucers. "And—oh—to get this quickly out of the way, the rehearsal went dismally. I dropped out of the play. A bunch of amateurs. The balcony I was supposed to jump from collapsed as soon as I stepped on it—"

I tried to laugh, but emitted only a squeak. Embarrassed, I cleared my throat.

"She is slipping. I always sensed she was a little kinky, but never to the point of this kind of humiliation." Patricia stared thoughtfully into her tea, put it down, then picked up a book. She seemed to be leafing through it, but I knew she was thinking about what I had told her. Across her inwardly turned eyes I could see the images moving from my words into her private dream world, where they would be transformed in a way I could never fathom.

Jake barked. I went to the door. Jake always started barking fifteen minutes before a guest arrived. I had asked Frank to stop by this evening. Earlier, in the backyard, he had seemed downcast, staring at the sky as though praying for rain. I thought he might need company.

Patricia looked up as I came back to the couch. "False alarm."

She smiled. She had a smear of lipstick on her front teeth; she had been biting her lip.

"So what do you think? Am I being crazy or what?"

"Crazy, sure, to climb up the balcony. He could have seen you, and had you arrested. Or you might have fallen and broken your neck." Jake had come up and laid his wet muzzle on her lap. Patricia petted his head distractedly. "About the rest, I don't know. I haven't slept soundly since he moved in, if I must be completely honest. I try to avoid him whenever I can, for no good reason. We don't speak much beyond the formal hello, how are you, weather's been pretty weird. That kind of thing. But he stares and doesn't see—or something. I swear he must have false eyelashes. His face looks like a picture of a face, but the eyes don't follow you, like in the traditional gothic scenario." She stopped abruptly; her left hand balled into a fist, the thumb clenched inside.

The doorbell rang. Jake went crazy, slid into the hall, and crashed into the door.

I held Jake back with one leg and let Frank in. He carried a pizza and another package on top of the box. "Thought you might be hungry," he said. "You provide the beer." He walked morosely into the living room.

"Oh, hi, Patricia, I hope I'm not interrupting anything."

"Interrupting? No, come join the fun. We're dissecting the neighbors, one in particular." Patricia looked up meaningfully at the ceiling.

"Oh, him . . ." Frank blushed, went into the kitchen to put down the pizza.

He came out with the small package in his outstretched hands, carrying it as though it might bite.

"Speaking of Paul Marks—a very good-looking fellow, but a little slick." Frank was from the Midwest. "I just ran into him in the hall, outside his door. He gave me this." And Frank handed the package to me.

"He said it was for you."

Patricia leaned forward anxiously. The box was wrapped in heavy brown paper and twine. I got the scissors and cut the package open.

Inside was a pair of opera glasses.

* * *

I told Frank the whole story. He and I wolfed down the pizza and a six-pack; Patricia smoked an especially fragrant joint.

"A little opium," she explained. "Clears my nervous system."

"Well, I guess he did see you," Patricia said. Anger crept into her voice, a slow steady wave. "He was performing for your benefit—as well as for his friends'. I should talk—I love an audience too. I bet he videotaped it."

Frank looked numb, kept straightening his crotch. I leaned down to tie my shoe, and noticed that Frank was fighting down a guilty erection.

"What a prick!" I shouted suddenly, loud enough so that any listening ears upstairs could hear. I opened the living-room window and shouted at the shivering leaves, "What a prick!"

"Cool down, Michael," Patricia said. "We don't want an open war here."

I paced back and forth in front of the window, sampling the breeze. My sinuses were stuffy, the first sign of a change of weather. Was the barometer falling?

I watched my reflection pace; I did so without self-consciousness: I would usually not allow others to observe me observing myself.

"Why am I so upset?" I said. Frank looked up sympathetically, wanting to have an answer for me but too far sunk in his own problems.

"Maybe your masculine pride is wounded," Patricia suggested. "Opera glasses. Effeminate. And that unreal fucking machine upstairs. You down here listening to his every move, his every command."

At the word "command" my hackles rose. Yet I knew that once again Patricia had hit the mark.

Frank gave me a spiritless hug at the front door. "I should go," he said sadly. "I'm afraid I'm not much fun tonight." He shuffled his feet. "Or help."

He started to go, then turned back. Patricia called from the hall, " 'Night, boys. And, Frank, thanks for the pizza."

I grabbed Frank's tense arm. Tremors. "Frank, what's going on? You're upset."

"It shows? My wife used to say she could never tell how I was feeling."

I laughed. "My wife used to say the same thing. After a while, I became convinced that I wasn't feeling anything. Maybe I'm not. I've got one more beer in the fridge. We can split it, and you can tell me what's on your mind."

"Okay, it might help."

I poured the beer into two glasses. Frank's chest heaved—badly contained emotion; I felt it in my own chest.

"My son, Brian," he began. "You remember Brian. You met him in the hall. Cut his finger? That one."

I told him I remembered. "How was the zoo?"

"The zoo was awful. Brian was awful. He kept running up to people and asking them if they were his real parents." Frank looked puzzled. "I didn't know what to do, so I took him home. His mother was out for the day, so I found a neighbor girl to baby-sit until Peg got home. Peg and Brian now live in our house—in my house—and I live in this crummy apartment with rattling windows."

I nodded sympathetically. I was used to being single now; in fact, I had started to like it. But Dorothy and I had not had children to constantly remind us of the ties that do not bind.

"Anyway, two days later Peg called me and said she had to go overseas for a year, a job assignment she couldn't turn down. She wants me to take care of Brian while she's gone. She's subletting the house, and asked me ... no, told me Brian could move in here with me. Here! I told her it was too small, that Brian was acting weird, but she was a brick wall. Once she's made up her mind, there's not getting through to her."

"Why don't you move back into the house yourself, while she's gone? At least you'd have more room. Although I wouldn't like to see you go."

Frank smiled for the first time this evening. "Thanks. But Peg doesn't want me in the house; she as much as said so. It's hers now, the courts gave it to her, and she's sticking to the letter of the law. And we have joint custody over Brian, so what she's asking me to do about him is legal too, strictly speaking, though we never talked about actually sharing him half and half—too confusing for him to have two homes."

"It'll work out," I said lamely. "Maybe you and Brian can get to know each other again."

"I already know Brian," Frank said darkly.

"When is he moving in?"

Frank got up, walked toward the door, Jake following him. "Next weekend." He stood in the hall for a moment. "Thanks for listening."

A sudden wind had come up. Then there was a sound of pattering on the glass, like thrown sand.

I looked out. It was starting to rain.

I dreamt automatons.

I needed the comfort of the indifferent solitude of nature. I went to the park. The park was full of creatures who looked like people but who walked stiffly, eyes fixed straight ahead. Each of them had a dog on a leash.

There was something wrong with all of them, despite their perfect mechanical movements. On closer examination, one youthful-looking man had mottled skin and was twenty years older than he had seemed, another wore an elevated shoe, there were several amputees and hunchbacks cleverly disguised, dwarfs positioned beside small trees to make them appear normal height, and so on. You had to look twice to be sure.

There was only one exception. He was perfect, unseamed, unblemished, full, and seemingly fit. He was the tallest of the tall, and walked with a restrained swagger that denoted power and control: the leader of the pack. He held a small red box in his hands, and when he twisted the buttons, the people moved.

I turned and ran. He twisted a button. I stopped.

"I did not give you permission to leave," he said in a voice dry like chalk.

I was frozen. Blue flies swarmed over me, settled on the exposed parts of my body, and began to bite.

The man smiled. Twisted some knobs.

The defective automatons were now tearing at themselves. The dogs were barking riotously, and broke their leashes.

The man's smile broadened as he frantically twisted the knobs. Slowly the defective ones came apart around me, falling to the ground, while I stood still at the center, black with insects, which soon covered my eyes and blinded me.

It had rained all night. I got up, looked at myself in the mirror. Who was that small, wizened sleep-drowned creature?

Not me.

I shook my head to try to clear it of the dream, but it would not leave. Falling to the floor, I managed fifty sloppy push-ups; got up, frustrated, kneading alien muscles, then fell to the floor again and did the push-ups right.

Sleep, I thought, while making coffee, sleep steals your soul at night, and you have to fight to get it back when you awaken.

Standing in front of the mirror with my first cup of coffee, I watched the edges of my sleep-blurred form redefine, my back straighten, and the image I knew as Michael come back into focus. I winked, I flirted; then smiled at myself smiling at myself.

As I turned away, I felt uncomfortable, really alone. I had learned to like being alone. It was less complicated. The sudden desolation puzzled me. I looked back at the mirror to see if I was still there.

For a moment the mirror was empty.

Then my image slid back into place.

It was late morning. I knocked at her door. I had to know more.

I kept knocking until I heard footsteps, a muffled curse, then she pulled back the gray blind.

She looked at me coldly, like I was a solicitor. She dropped the blind, mumbled something. I leaned against the wall to wait.

In five minutes she returned, opened the door; she blocked the opening with her body, one hand snaking around the doorframe.

"Michael, what an unexpected surprise," she said dully, with no attempt at being charming. "Come in."

"Oh, cut the crap, Janette. I'm not one of those people you lead around by the nose."

She looked shocked, and I thought I saw a momentary breakdown in the chill, but the wall between us quickly reformed.

"Do I smell coffee?" I asked, deciding the best tactic would be to wait, feel my way around her, then bring up the subject of Paul Marks.

"Yes, coffee, I'll get you some." She wore a sea-blue bathrobe and in the deep prismatic light thrown by the rain, she looked unaccountably lovely; tousled hair gleaming, eyes as deep blue as her robe, tan ankles, a faint blond fuzz on the nape of her neck that traced down to a gently curving spine, like a crescent moon.

"Finally," I said, taking the steaming cup from her while she avoided my eyes and stared out the window into the streaming air well, "a break in the weather. I thought the winter would never get started. We've got eight months of dirty air to clear out."

"I hate the rain," she said. "It reminds me of England. In England it rains all the bloody time. You could turn into a mushroom."

I laughed. She did not.

I put the coffee cup down on the glass coffee table. The couch was white leather. There was a Persian rug, dark red, and brass lamps, huge polished globes on slender stalks that reminded me of insects and overhung the sides of the couch.

I sat in the middle.

After a time I called to her: "Janette, you have a guest who is eagerly awaiting your company."

She threw some pots around; then there was a loud sigh,

and she erupted from the kitchen, an unenthusiastic smile on her face.

Outside, the rain was thundering down. The room darkened as clouds rolled in from the north.

Janette turned on the brass lamps, flooding the room with light. Then she pulled the curtains.

"Your guest likes the rain. But I suppose it's not important what I like—"

"Oh, shut up," she said suddenly. "You are fucking persistent today." She leaned down to straighten a pillow; her robe parted, revealing a tender cleft in which hung a single pearl on a chain. I noticed, she noticed. She leaned further over.

"Enjoying the view?" she said rather bitterly.

I reached forward and tried to pull her robe together. Instead, the robe fell open further. Janette straightened, not attempting to close it. She looked defiant, like a stubborn child.

"Ouch," she said, pulling the robe from her shoulders. "I'm a little sore."

I walked around behind her.

Her back was streaked with red and blue lines, as though someone had pulled strong fingers along her skin; there were no scratches, just long bruises.

"Don't you say a word, not a bloody word," she said.

I kept quiet for a minute while she gingerly fastened her robe.

"Janette, what do you see in the guy?" I exploded. "You may not know it, but I can hear you downstairs."

"And this from you"—she was almost shouting—"after what you put me through." She burst into tears and ran from the room.

I went after her, and found myself face-to-face with the closed bathroom door, which was a two-sided mirror. Pressed against myself, I mumbled, "Janette, what do you mean, put you through?"

"The first night—the only night—we slept together."

I had a sick sensation in my stomach. I wanted to leave but could not. Instead, I tried the door; she had not locked it. She was sitting on the edge of the bathtub. I knelt down and held her for a moment; her tears fell on my shoulder.

When she had calmed down a little, I repeated my question. She looked up with swollen eyes.

Then in a quiet voice she told me of our first night together, the night I had forgotten.

"You don't remember it, do you?" Janette asked. "No, I can see you don't. Maybe some things are better left unremembered. But you asked for it.

"I brought you flowers. We had champagne," she said. "They always remember the champagne. We got tipsy, did a little necking on the couch, and I—fool that I am—suggested we move into the bedroom."

Slowly, she was getting control of herself. "It's a shame you don't remember—at least this part. I did quite a professional strip-tease on the way into the bedroom, dropping a piece of clothing at every step. You were panting by the time we made it to the bed.

"I was busy with my seduction, you know, so I hadn't looked at your face for a minute or two. But when I did, you had changed. Your expression was . . . vacant, but sort of hungry.

"It made me nervous, but I had gone in too far to back out. You looked like you would burst. We lay down on the bed, and then you jumped on me. I don't want to get graphic, but I really don't like getting fucked in the mouth so hard I can't breathe.

"I pushed you away. Then you said wait a minute, climbed off, and ran into the kitchen. You came back in with a big butcher knife in your hands.

"I tried to get up but you pushed me back down and I hit my head, not too hard, but I couldn't think straight for a couple of seconds. You put the knife on the bedside table. You crawled back into bed. I was about ready to kick you in the face, when you said—and I remember this word for word:

"'Don't be afraid. The knife is only there in case you want to use it.'"

I didn't do much but go to work, sleep, talk with the neighbors, and drink. I had been warned about the dangers of drinking alone, but somehow I didn't feel alone.

Janette's description of our night together drove me into an even deeper isolation: I was skulking through the building once again, like a thief, trying to avoid contact. Apparently I was some sort of guilty criminal, an amnesiac.

The doorbell rang a few times; probably Patricia or Frank. I heard a new voice in the hallway: Frank's son, Brian, who apparently had moved in a few days earlier.

I spent most evenings in bed, with a bottle of brandy, trying to unravel the mystery.

I've always been a victim of postcoital depression. Dorothy could never understand why, when we were finished making love, I rushed to the bathroom, locked the door, and took a long shower.

Dorothy would say that sex made her feel good, satisfied, a little sleepy, dreamy.

When I come, I feel I have lost something.

I became convinced that that sense of loss had something to do with my intimate encounter with Janette.

Over the next few days I formulated a theory. I surmised that the man who had brought the knife from the kitchen had not been myself, but the materialized form of some deep fear that I had yet to uncover. Perhaps grief at the divorce. It sounded good, clinical.

Therefore, I reasoned, I was not fully responsible for what had transpired. We are only responsible for what we think, not what we are.

I knew it would not do any good to tell Janette this—she wasn't hot on theory. Instead, the next time I saw her, I would apologize for running out of the apartment the other night, and apologize further for not being entirely myself on our first encounter.

Maybe she'd give me a second chance.

The weather pattern shifted for a week, and the edges of the storms reached us, though it was a mizzling rain for the most part, except for a couple of brief squalls.

Then the silent eye of the storm front locked us in again. There was clear blue sky for two days, and then the yellow haze returned. Tule fog rose from the ground at night, blurring the division between land and sky.

I stared out my window at the mist hovering over the swimming pool, and saw myself lost somewhere in the hidden dividing line.

Upstairs, the party continued, with only brief intervals of silence. The first night had been only the beginning; not an exception, but the rule. Paul Marks was rolling. Like sound effects in a movie, the sounds were too loud, unreal. I kept imagining a man shaking a sheet of metal.

My nerves grew ragged.

There was an endless parade of visitors. Strange feet whispered, thudded, shouted. There was only one pair that I recognized—Janette's—and she was his most frequent visitor.

You would think she'd had enough.

The depth of my isolation lasted a week. I didn't talk to anyone but the people at work.

At the end of the week I rummaged through my kitchen drawer and found the knife. It was a ridiculously long knife, like the one in *Psycho*. They made these things for movies, not real life.

I put the knife next to my bed. I lay down and fell into a peaceful sleep, the first in a long time.

"Frank and I were starting to get worried." I had waited until Patricia passed by my door, then followed her down the stairs. At the bottom of the stairway, the light from the front door produced a halo around her hair; her face was dark.

"I was in a funk, a real bad one," I said, joining her at the foot of the stairs. "Janette and I talked out our problem." A half-truth. "But there was some stuff at work too: it was intimated that I had stolen—borrowed—money from petty cash. And the weather—I was hoping for more rain."

"You don't sound very convincing. Pardon my bluntness. And you're looking a little pale. Are you dyeing your hair, or is it the light?"

I shook my head.

"But I know what you mean—wanting to get away from it all, if that's what you mean. Pardon my hasty interpretation. We all have to leave mother earth now and then." She waited for a moment. "But I have to run now. An AIDS play. Audition. Maybe I'll stop over later, if your light is on."

I nodded.

"I'd very much like to," she said, "if it's not too late. She opened the door and she was gone.

Later that day I ran into the man upstairs.

Fortunately, maybe miraculously, I had seen him only once since our second encounter, honking and waving as he drove off in a silver Corvette. I had pretended to discipline Jake so that I would not have to respond.

Today the weather was tepid; the ground fog had taken its rightful place in the sky by midafternoon. I went down by the pool and sat.

Where I found evidence of a child. A toy tractor, red, one wheel broken off; a clown doll whose button eyes were missing; chalk marks for hopscotch, with a skull and cross-bones.

My heart went out to Frank. I knew what he must be going through now that Brian had moved in. Frank's apartment was messy, but he knew where everything was in the apparent disorder. Once we had been talking about an album and he had reached down into a pile of several hundred records and pulled out the right one without searching.

A private alphabet.

Lost in thought, I watched my image rippling on the disturbed surface of the pool. There were leaves floating across my eyes. I was about to get the net and clean off the surface when a hand fell on my shoulder, holding me down.

"Michael, isn't it?" came the even-tempered voice.

A public alphabet.

My heart sank. I stood up, even though he had not removed his hand. I felt in some way that he was pulling me up. He had a horrible calm authority. "Yes, Michael. Hello, Paul? Paul Marks. I see you on the mailbox, often. Funny we haven't run into each other more."

Paul looked at me quizzically, as though my words were bullets failing to penetrate bulletproof glass. His eyes were glazed, unmoving, beautiful in their way.

"Did you get my gift? Frank said he'd pass it along."

I bristled. "Yes, though I am a little confused. Opera glasses?"

"Janette said you were into opera. Not my style. I'm more a pop man myself. I found them when I was moving, someone had brought them to a party for a joke, and left them. I thought you might like them."

I could not read his expression. Had he seen me hanging outside his window?

"Janette," I said in a careful even voice, "must have been pulling your leg. I don't like opera either. Don't like music much at all anymore. Though I used to." This last seemed like a confession; I immediately regretted it.

"Well, the joke's on both of us." He paused, fingering

the cleft in his chin. "I can see your shadow on the sidewalk below, and know you do a lot of watching. Well, maybe you can use the glasses for something a little more interesting than opera. That redhead across the way, for example."

"What a shame! A tree blocks my view from my living-room window, and that big palm at the back of the yard stops me from seeing into the apartments across the way." I really could see in, a little. Lying to him, I realized, gave me pleasure.

"Oh, really," he said. "I guess I'm lucky to be upstairs. I'm above the trees."

"Well, nice running into you. Told the landlord I'd clean up the pool," I said. I went to the gazebo, got the net, and began fishing out leaves.

"See you soon," I said, because he hadn't budged. Then he was off, square head, triangular sweep to a narrow waist; upstairs and away in a single bound. A twinge of jealousy rose through me, like nausea.

"Soon," he promised from the alley, and disappeared.

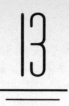

"**H**orrible, horrible, horrible." Patricia was drinking a Dos Equis from the bottle. It was almost midnight.

"And I thought I had had a bad day . . . week . . . lifetime," I said sympathetically, relieved at last to be thinking about something other than myself.

"Those people, smarmy beyond belief, aspiring writers of verses for greeting cards. Or cold—cool—beyond belief. Am I repeating myself? They have no idea that they're dull as mud. The worst kind of crazy." She stared ahead blankly, as though she had picked up some of the disease she was describing. When she had finished half the bottle, her eyes grew warm again; emerald green, the color of seawater over coral reefs.

"Well we're all actors to some extent," I said, trying to be fair.

"Oh, not everybody is destined for that particular torment. There are imitators, and clever mimics, and some not so clever. But real actors know that they are acting, or at least they know a good part from a bad one." She spoke vehemently, spraying beer on her hand, which she had been waving in the air like a flag. "Oops, sorry," she said, wiping her hand delicately on her skirt. "Finding a character is like trying to find water in a deep well. Is the rope long enough? Will it hold? Is there really anything there?" She stared morosely at her lap, then leaned over and gave me a moist kiss on my cheek. "Surprise. We're just people. I guess we'll survive."

"Some of us are just people." I moved closer and put my arm around her; I felt a sudden protectiveness. "I remember a story I read when I was a kid," I said, "about a crazy deformed woman who made beautiful masks. The masks gave her the illusion of physical perfection, and she acted the part. She was really a killer. I think the outside world is like that now."

Patricia shivered, leaned on my shoulder. "And what happens," she said, "when someone rips off the mask—or it comes off of its own accord?"

"Then maybe we'll start to deal with the real face?" I said hopefully.

Patricia suddenly laughed, a fresh sound, like wind. "Or probably someone will construct an even more fiendish mask. Or convince us that what is beneath is really beautiful."

We laughed until our stomachs ached and our eyes were filled with tears.

Upstairs, came a pounding like pistons. It was steady, thoughtless, persistent, like an imbecile fucking. We ignored it at first, but soon we laughed a little less, then our smiles began to fade.

Was someone upstairs monitoring our every word?

I thought we must look like guilty children holding hands on the couch, waiting to be punished.

"And what about the sadist upstairs?" I asked. "Where does he fit into the picture?"

"Oh, he's quintessential, the spirit of the times," Patricia said thoughtfully. She got another beer, and potato chips, and settled back into her place, still warm from her body.

She sat up suddenly. "I've got an idea. Let's go out together this weekend. To a club. Do some major mask ripping. And get ripped, as it were." Beer was running down her chin; I mopped it with a napkin and took a sip from her glass. I savored the sweet taste of her saliva on the rim, and the oily pungency of her lipstick.

"But where?" I asked. I had tried out a couple of clubs recently and had been turned away at the door for not wearing the right clothes. "I'm always at the wrong place at the right time."

"Oh, I know a perfectly awful place, full of attitude." She craned her neck forward and her eyes grew deliberately blank. "Club Nouveau. Very exclusive. Strict door policy. But I know the doorman; he used to be an all-right guy, before he got into cocaine. Money is his thing now. And people with money. Awful drug. I much prefer opiates. Evidence of God on earth, instead of locomotion." She smiled widely, revealing perfect white teeth in which I could see my reflection.

I didn't know exactly what she meant, but didn't care; I felt an upwelling of friendship, a warm disturbing wave, and I thought I would follow her to the ends of the earth if she asked.

"So are you up for it, Mr. Isolation? Saturday night. In our finest?"

"Okay, sure, it sounds fun. If the ambience isn't right—"

"And you can depend on that—" Patricia added.

"Then we'll rip 'em to shreds."

Frank was sitting by the pool. I could see him through the twitching leaves as they scratched across my windowpane. His head was on his knees. He was shirtless and it looked like his back muscles were twitching.

At first I thought it was a new form of exercise; then I realized he was crying.

"Frank," I yelled down from the window, to give him time to pull himself together. "I'll be down in a minute."

The window upstairs closed. Paul Marks had been watching. I felt a chill. Frank seemed so vulnerable sometimes. Did Paul have Frank in mind for a little surgery? Perhaps to remove the physical evidence of grief?

I walked through the darkening window well. It was twilight. I looked up. Four stories of kitchen windows, below a square of sky, pinkish-blue. Afraid that Paul Marks would join us by the pool—he was insatiably sociable, judging from the number of people who had passed through his place already—I moved quietly.

Frank had pulled on his shirt and taken his feet from the pool. Patricia dangled her feet, I learned from her, and now Frank had the habit. Everything moves in a circle.

He turned at my approach. His eyes were a little puffy. "You look hung-over," I said.

"Yeah, bad night. Sit down." He patted the concrete.

I gave his neck a quick squeeze; I could feel the emotions trembling under my fingers. The tendons were like ropes.

"How's your son—Brian, wasn't it?"

"Yeah. He moved in this week. Where have you been? Haven't seen you around. Hiding from anyone in particular?"

"From myself mostly," I said. Frank had such a hangdog look, I wondered briefly if he thought I had been avoiding him. "Had an anxiety attack, and didn't feel like I wanted to be seen. Sorry if I've been negligent."

Frank's eyes brightened. "Do you have these ... ah ... attacks often?"

"Only since Dorothy and I got divorced. Most of the time I like being alone. But once in a while I start feeling desperate and then I have no choice but to stay inside, I'm such a needy mess. If you know what I mean."

Frank cleared his throat. "Do I know? Happens to me all the time. Don't know what I'm going to do now that Brian is here. He's always demanding something, and won't let me be."

"Is that why you're sitting back here?" I asked.

"Sort of—but mostly thinking about Peg, how she always did this kind of thing to me. Wouldn't let me have my moods. Now she's got Brian to do it for her." He threw his hands up in the air. "I don't know. Brian is like his mother—an invader from another planet."

"Dorothy and I didn't have any children. I didn't want to. That was one of the big problems."

Frank leaned forward, all bunched up, until it seemed he would fall into the pool. He stared at his reflection. "My hair's almost gone. Past my prime. Set in my ways. I wonder how I'll ever get through this year."

Then Frank's back started to heave a little under the gray sweatshirt.

"Oh, you'll adjust. It'll just take some time," I said hurriedly, pounding him on the back to knock the feeling back inside him.

"So tell me about you and Dorothy," he said. "I'm sick of my problems."

There used to be nothing I enjoyed doing more than rehashing my relationship with Dorothy. Roger, a friend at work, had lunch with me almost every day when I was deep in the crisis, and listened to me carry on for months.

And I would have imaginary conversations with Dorothy in my head for almost a year after the divorce was final. The memories of the relationship were so strong they made real people and situations seem ghostly at times.

"Well," I said musingly. "Let's see." Nothing came to mind.

Where are you hiding, Dorothy?

"If you don't want to, don't . . ." Frank looked pathetic, his eyes like a bloodhound's; some of the feeling I had had for Dorothy rose up again.

"We met in college," I said finally. I was studying English, then went into medicine, then switched to marine biology. I got an M.S. in that, started my doctorate, but never finished. Seemed useless to be so motivated, when you're in love. Know what I mean? I had gotten what I was after, or so I thought. We were like two parts of the same person, Dorothy and me. An instant chemical thing. I couldn't have gotten away if I tried. Like trying to avoid your reflection in the mirror." Frank was still staring into the pool. He had put his feet back in.

"Go on, I'm listening," he said. I moved closer to him.

"Well, we moved to the Bay Area, East Bay at first, then San Francisco. I had felt bad about not finishing my Ph.D., but when I got here and saw so many educated people going nowhere, I didn't feel so bad. Dorothy and I both worked at UCSF for a while, glorified clerical work, had a nice flat, which we got paid to leave when the building was sold. That place in Cole Valley was home. Somehow, our relationship was that place. When we moved into Noe Valley, we were never the same again. In my mind I kept thinking back to the times we had had back then, over there. Somehow everything was suddenly behind me." I paused. "I'm not boring you? Once I get started on this stuff, I can go on for days."

"No, really."

"That was when Dorothy decided she wanted to have a baby. I had gone on to a second job, but Dorothy was still at UCSF, an administrative position. Lots of money, but the pressure was driving her hormones crazy. I had taken a job at a psych hospital, low pay, because I thought it would be interesting material. I still had the idea that one day I would write a novel, and what better place to gather material. Dorothy was making three times the money I was. But who cared? We were modern. We had always been pretty equal in all things, sexual roles, all that. No power struggles to speak of. Sex was sometimes a little dull, but you have to put up with that in a long-term relationship."

"Amen," Frank said, kicking up waves.

"Anyway, Dorothy got more demanding about getting pregnant. She worried she was getting old, it was more dangerous every year. I disagreed. Things are different now; people are waiting longer. Anyway, the subject of a child became the—let me wax poetic—the reef on which the ship of our relationship wrecked."

"Maybe you should forget the novel," Frank said, smiling suddenly. I tried to laugh.

"Did you love her?" Frank asked, looking me steadily in the eyes.

I rubbed my chin. I felt dizzy. At last I said, "I don't

know. I suppose I thought I did. Now I can't even remember her face." I closed my eyes and tried.

There was a sudden breeze, movement between Frank and me. Lost in myself, I did not look up.

"No," I said, "I don't think I ever even knew her."

When I opened my eyes, Brian was sitting between us, staring at me with the hostile fascination of a jealous lover.

Big sensuous lips over mine. Hot breath in my face, fragrant with perspiration from my own groin. Rigid muscles like armor, sliding through the wetness. Something large between us, big as a billy club, crawling up my chest, covered with skin which moved up and down the shaft like cloth.

I struggled, was held down. Soon I was overpowered, though fit to burst with anticipation, with crazy desire. Come on, do it, I'm ready; tell me who I am.

Then with a single thrust he was inside me, horrible at first, then a sort of overload of pleasure that was like pain shot up my spine, knocked all thoughts out of me. More, I wanted more; I wanted everything. I could see the swift strokes of his penis from back to front, as though it fitted into the glove of my own erection, which I now stroked.

I woke slowly, fitfully, trying to shrug off the weight. Guiltily I clawed my way to consciousness, running my fingers down his back, tearing flesh.

When my fingers were wet with blood and sweat, I woke.

I turned over onto my side, felt the cold wet spot.

Watched the man return to the mirror.

"Good morning, Michael," I said. He climbed back into the mirror and began to mimic my motions.

"Brian, be careful. Jake sometimes gets a little wild when he's with someone other than me. Be sure to use the leash,"

I said, handing it to him. Brian looked at the leather lead distastefully.

"Sure, whatever you say," he said. In the fluorescent hall light Brian's veins showed through his pale skin like a road map.

I reminded myself to be more forgiving. He was the product of a broken home. He'd be an adult with problems. He'd go to therapy and come out the same.

But it wasn't his fault.

He had taken to Jake, my lovable moronic dog. They made a good pair. I let him walk Jake whenever he wanted, which so far had been about a half-dozen times. It was the least I could do for Frank, to let him have a little time alone.

"Brian," I said. "You've met Dr. Marks, haven't you? My upstairs neighbor?"

"Yeah, what of it?" Brian looked guilty, then angry. "How'd you know? You been listening?"

"I just thought I heard you a couple of times. Once it was kind of late. Some people are trying to sleep. Does your father know?"

"Know what?" Brian said. "I talk to everybody. Dad doesn't want to talk. He's always depressed. So I have new friends."

He took Jake down the stairs, slamming the front door on his way out and almost catching Jake's tail. I was about to go after him, but didn't have the energy.

"Frank, do you think it's a good idea for Brian to be spending time with you-know-who?" I asked, finishing the last sip of coffee, which was full of grounds.

Frank looked puzzled. He had begun to put on a little weight. Brian had been living with him almost six weeks. The bold musculature only accentuated the extra fat. Frank noticed my glance, patted his stomach. "I can take it off in a week. Brian eats up so much time, I'm off my exercise schedule. And Brian likes chocolate. It keeps him quiet and happy, which God knows I can't manage. But when he's at school, I sometimes get into the stuff myself. Don't have much other fun anymore."

He had ignored my question. I repeated: "Have you noticed that Brian is spending a lot of time upstairs ..." I motioned with my head. "I've even started hearing him late at night."

"What big ears you have ..." Frank said, laughing weakly. "I hadn't noticed. I saw them talking in the hall together once. I try to avoid the guy, he gives me the creeps." Then a look of worry crossed Frank's face; a classic case of delayed reaction. "At night?"

"I'm sure I know Brian's step; you get to know a lot when you have someone over you, moving constantly. I don't think anybody in that apartment ever sits down. It must be some kind of law that once you pass his doorway, you are forever in motion. Sort of like the damned in hell, constantly milling about."

"Michael, honestly, I don't know. My mind has been so occupied, trying to do the right thing, I've been in a fog. Do you think there's anything weird going on? I mean, perverted?"

That thought hadn't crossed my mind. You read about those kinds of things all the time, but they seem far away, the fresh graves of children they are always finding, the abuse of innocence that takes place right under your nose and you never know who.

"No, I doubt it. He has a string of girlfriends, including Janette. Sometimes he sleeps with more than one at a time ..."

Frank's eyes widened with surprise. "How do you know that?"

Thinking quickly, I said, "He boasted about it to me once. 'Sorry,' he said, 'if I kept you up last night, but I had twins over and we were up playing all night.'"

I didn't think it necessary to tell Frank that I had been hanging half the night from the balcony, watching, waiting, like an insect caught in a web.

* * *

I stood in front of the mirror. There was no doubt about it. My hair was turning dark. My mother had warned me that it would; I was the only blond in the family. She had waited for this moment all her life, to cover up what I suspected was an indiscretion with a certain blond gentleman while my father had been away at sea.

I would talk to her on Mother's Day. If I was feeling generous I would tell her, and set her mind at rest. Not that Dad would care; he was long since dead, felled by a hunter's bullet.

I had been ten years old. At his funeral his face was small, unimposing, surrounded by red silk, which looked wet. When I touched it, it had been dry and scratchy.

Dad always seemed like a loaded gun ready to go off. But in the end, the gun got him.

I tried to understand, to know what he meant when he looked at me—such a hard look. Always the same hard look.

I touched the surface of the mirror; my image did also. He was clever, moving in an exact pantomime. You'd have thought there was only one of us if you didn't know better.

I ran my fingers through my darkening hair. He did the same.

I wondered what he did when I wasn't looking.

Then I thought it better not to ask questions that couldn't be answered.

15

I knocked on Janette's door. The blind hung crookedly, so I could just barely see in. Janette came from the shadows, a ragged shape like splattered blood; a beam of light threw her face into relief. The features were drawn, angry. One eye gleamed with hatred; the other looked tired.

As she approached the door, her face changed. She put on her best Janette; suddenly, all evidence of conflict was erased, as though an invisible makeup artist were working on her in those twenty feet of empty hallway.

"Oh, God," she said, looking over my shoulder, "I must look terrible."

"Not now," I said.

"Huh?" she asked, but did not pursue it. She hugged me. "It's good to see you. I mean it. I've been needing to talk—but I've been too busy to make the effort."

"I thought you were through with me. I don't know how you can stand to look me in the face."

"Oh, no, I'm getting used to it," she said.

"Used to what?"

"To your face. To understanding nothing. Not myself. Not other people. Sometimes this bloody game wears me thin." She rubbed her hands over her features, which were pliable like soft rubber. "Just a minute, I'm going to wash off this makeup."

When she came back, she was scrubbed clean. "Now I feel like a person again. You know, I used to be the ugliest little girl. Tall, practically as tall as I am now when I was twelve. Big nose. You probably hadn't noticed; it's still big, but I grew into it a bit, and learned to play off it."

"Don't give me that," I said. "You've always been beautiful."

"No, honestly. I had a face that would stop a clock. When I was about sixteen I learned that you could control things if you acted in a certain way, presented yourself in a certain way. I read this book about behavior in public places, which reduces it all to an equation. When you start to play, and see how easy it is and how big the rewards are, it's like a drug. Who wants to feel bad, when it's so easy to feel good?"

"So why no makeup now?" As I looked at her more carefully, her features were somewhat rough, not the delicate pastel beauty her finished face portrayed. And there was an attractive masculinity to her looks which I had not noticed before.

"It's a strain to keep it up all the time. I just want to be a tomboy again, wrestle with the boys, beat them up. You don't know what a weight this is, this feminine thing. Sometimes I'd like to chuck it all, tell the world about Margaret and me. But now, with Paul, the best player of all"—a look of love, disgust, and pain crossed her features, fused it into a mask, then melted away—"I'm in a battle to the death. I can't resist a challenge, and he has set me off, after an initial loss of bearings."

"Oh, him," I said flatly. I didn't know what to say. "What I wanted to talk about was that problem of ours," I said, each word falling out like a stone.

Janette smiled. "I guess I shouldn't hold you responsible for the blackout. God knows I've blacked out more than once when sex was involved. Just recently, in fact." She winced, touching what must have been a sore arm under a blue-and-gray sweatshirt. "Though I think you might talk to someone professional about your sexual problem. Someday you might find someone who will use the knife." She scratched her chin. "On the other hand, if it's about trust, which I guess it is, you probably choose your partners carefully, so they won't use it. You don't seem like a suicidal maniac to me."

Her words were suddenly far away, like a bad phone connection.

I leaned over the polished surface of the table. I could almost hear a voice from there: This aspect of reality is taboo. Michael, you must ignore it.

The faraway feeling grew slowly, over thirty seconds, like a stranger coming up on you in the dark and putting his hands over your eyes. Dry winter, everything so far away. I sank into it so very easily. Even my heartbeat sounded like it came from somewhere else.

"Michael!" Janette scolded. "At least give me the courtesy of pretending you're listening."

"Uh . . . sorry." She looked blurry now, red and smudgy, angry but unreal. I shook my head, rubbed my eyes. Sight came back a little, and with it a concerned, slightly perturbed Janette.

"Oh, dear, you really don't remember about the knife, do you?" She leaned over suddenly and kissed my cheek, then pulled me into the warm curve of her arm. "Once, I had an uncle who molested me. It took me years to remember it, then years more to be able to say it out loud. Some things hurt too much to face, but at some point they hurt more not to face. So then you have a smaller pain to contend with; and get on with it."

I looked at her blankly; my reflection in the window, over her shoulder, was brittle. I smiled wanly; he did not.

"Well, let's not talk about it quite yet. When I'm ready. I promise."

"Okay, but don't let it get too crazy."

Sleeping next to the knife was as effective as a sleeping pill. Without it I was awake all night, staring at the ceiling.

A little later, when the difficult subject had been dropped, I ventured into her problem area. "Well, how about you and Paul Marks? Why did you ever get involved with him? He hurts you, I know it."

Janette frowned. Her muscles tensed, but she did not pull away.

"Well, that's a little too complicated to talk about now." Her voice was curiously flat, her eyes dreamy. "Something in him pulls me. Maybe it's a challenge to defeat him at his own game. Or maybe it's his big dick." She attempted a laugh, failed.

"What about Margaret? How's she fit in?"

Janette bolted upright. "She has nothing to do with this," she said vehemently. She got up and paced.

"You'll be meeting Margaret at the building barbecue. Billy gave out the invitations today." Billy lived downstairs; gay, worked in a bank, made me a little nervous. I liked to think of him as aloof, but in fact it might have been me.

"A barbecue in the middle of winter? Come on."

Janette pointed out the window. Dry as a bone out there. A dusty tree picked up the sunlight, sent swarms of fireflies across the floor.

"It's in a few days, look under your door for the announcement. *Everyone* is going to be there."

Brian was becoming a pest. He waited in the lobby for me to get home from work. Jumping out at me like a shadow with a life of its own, he would demand to see Jake, in that loud whining voice.

More for Frank's sake than anything, I gave in to Brian's demands. Kids are tyrants. What harm could come of it?

Eventually, however, I began to miss those twilight walks with Jake, the chalky sky, the distant sun sinking below the black roofs.

"Brian, Jake's been acting weird lately," I said one evening when Brian came knocking. "You can take him tonight, but I think I'd better spend some more time with him after this. A dog needs one master. He's getting confused. Okay?" Why was I asking this child for permission?

Brian followed me up the stairs. I got Jake and the leash and sent them off.

I fell asleep in front of the evening news waiting for them to return.

Jake lay at the foot of the bed. He had started to growl, lowly.

"Shut up, Jake," I said. The growling intensified. Was someone coming to visit? I listened: drone of distant cars, an occasional voice wafting through the alley through my open window, leaves stirring in the breeze, and underscoring it all (as I listened more intently to the below sounds), a dull bass note.

"Shut up, Jake," I said. "I mean it." To no effect.

I coughed, now fully awake, and tried not to look into the mirror, because I had the sneaking suspicion, from the empty feeling in my gut, that my counterpart was not there.

I nestled into my damp arm and peered over anyway. A heap of reflected covers, two eyes staring redly, hopelessly out.

I raised my head. My reflection had no face. My—or his—eyes hung there disembodied, like a pair of strange marine-reef fish suspended in unmoving water.

I got up slowly, holding the covers around me for protection. I turned my back, headed toward the window and open air.

Jake slowly rose, his hackles up. He watched me glassily, as though I were a stranger. His back was arched, his head held down; he moved carefully in my direction, his growl now steady and threatening.

Something cold clamored through me, then out. I turned

around. It leapt in a blurry arc to the mirror, and in the blink of an eye my image was back, full-faced and complete.

Jake looked puzzled, shook his head as if to rid himself of a flea, then lay down with a sigh.

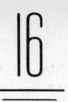

16

I hadn't realized how much time I had been spending inside alone. I worked, I ate, I shit, I seldom went out. Isolation had crept up on me slowly, like a sniper. Now that I was in his sights, I did not know which way to turn.

I covered my bedroom mirror with a curtain. Yet when I leaned over at night to turn out the light, I could see his face in the polished blade of the knife, which still lay on the bedside table to remind me.

Before I knew it, the day of the barbecue had arrived. And the next night I had agreed to go to Club Nouveau with Patricia.

Double exposure; double fear.

Twilight fell, voices rose from the backyard. There was splashing in the pool. Footsteps came from upstairs, paused before my door, then moved down. Two pairs, one belonging to Paul Marks, the other not in my catalog.

Brian's voice seemed to rattle the leaves outside my window, like a racing squirrel. I had let him take Jake down early, so he would stay out of Frank's hair.

I chose my outfit carefully, baggy gray pants, a white wedding jacket, white shoes.

Finally a voice yelled from below: "Hey, slowpoke, get on down here. Nobody is going to bite you." It was Frank, sounding a little drunk.

I composed myself. "Be right down," I said, trying to

sound amused. My voice quivered. I hoped the distance would eat it up.

All dressed up, then carefully down the stinking stairway, stairs sagging in the middle, past the garbage cans, then out into the fray. It's hard, I thought, to join a party when it has been going for a while. Like trying to merge into freeway traffic with an empty tank.

Wanting to be invisible, I slouched through people shapes toward the table where the bottles of liquor glowed like beacons.

Keeping my back turned, I filled a glass with brandy, drank it straight down.

"Michael, old pal, you're looking fit as a fiddle." Frank had circled from the rear; pounded me on the back, almost knocking the empty glass from my hand.

"Just getting ready," I said, turning slowly like a performer about to confront his audience.

I grabbed his hand, shook it hard. Sweaty, fleshy, real; I felt a little better. Frank's eyes were full of glittering intoxication, but warm and good-humored. An earthbound drunk.

Jake rubbed against my leg. I reached down to pet him. He growled, then moved under the table.

"So tell me who's on the agenda. I haven't had the courage to lift my eyes from my glass."

"Look up." He pointed. I obeyed. The backyard was decorated with paper globes, helium balloons filled too full (three had already broken), crepe paper hanging from the trees like the aftermath of a fraternity prank.

"Lovely," I said sarcastically. "Very artful."

"I beg your pardon. I helped with the decorations. Billy and I—"

"Just goes to show you that not all gay men have impeccable taste." I laughed.

"Boy, you are in a state. Maybe you should go back upstairs," Frank said.

"You and Billy?" I said. "How'd you get roped into that?"

"Don't be like that. Have another drink."

I poured brandy to the top of the glass, spilling it on my hand.

"Over there," Frank continued, "are people. Real people."

"Seriously?"

"You need to work off some of that aggression." He pointed with amused authority. "Over there are Billy and his friend, I've forgotten his name. And Patricia, you remember Patricia. And there"—Frank gestured with a fully outstretched arm—"are Paul Marks and his girlfriend. Forgot her name too. A real looker."

Paul's back was turned. He wore a baggy white sweater, knit shirt with the collar turned up, and pin-striped pants. I immediately regretted wearing white. His woman friend poised at his side as though a photographer were in the bushes.

"Kristy and Polly, in front of him." Frank started to laugh. "Lighten up, Michael. How long's it been since you've been to a party?"

Paul's friend had disengaged from his arm in one liquid turn. Director to actress: walk deliberately to the other side, let nothing distract you from your purpose.

She walked toward me, veered off at the last moment. Her eyes looked around, above, finally through me.

"Excuse me," she said, and I moved aside to clear access to the booze. She floated past like a sleepwalker. "Paul is thirsty."

I bit my tongue, thought of tripping her.

"Nice butt, but a little uppity for me," Frank muttered.

"I bet she's one of his protégées," I said. "I wonder what she looked like before he cut her up. A hunchback covered with hair, a drooling child with a twisted face, you know, a challenge to the surgeon's scalpel."

Patricia pulled herself from Paul's circle and half-skipped, half-floated toward us.

"The party's over there"—she pointed, then smirked. "He has an endless array of stories, anecdotes, all about how one maintains a successful veneer. The girl is one of his—"

Frank and I started to laugh. She looked puzzled.

"Michael was just saying—" Frank began.

"Well, Michael was right. And they're bragging about it. Turns out Polly has had a little cosmetic breast surgery too. Oh, the conversation is really spicy. I bowed out just in time. I could see Paul's eyes moving over my face, reshaping it." She took the drink from my hand and sipped. "No, thanks, doctor, I've learned to love my peculiarities."

"Seems to be attracting a lot of attention," I said. "Soon we'll all be over there, making appointments."

"Vaccuum does that, then you crash into it, can't get out . . ."

"And break apart," I said, enjoying watching Patricia's thoughts spiral.

"Okay, you guys, remember poor old Frank is here. Talk in English."

"Well, at any rate, it's good to see you out of your hole, Michael. I thought I might have to come up and drag you out. Might be the best thing for you—facing up to your fears, and all that." Patricia pointed at the broad back; Paul's head tilted, wobbled like a wooden doll's, but he held his body at rigid attention, his feet firmly planted. I felt a moment of deep sympathy; then I realized it was a sympathy I could not afford.

Feeling sheepish, I asked, "Where's Janette? Surely she's coming?"

"Oh, yes," Patricia said, tilting her glass to the sky, "and with her the fabled Margaret—or so she promised. Probably had to fix their makeup after a rousing bout of lovemaking."

"What do they do with each other?" Frank asked half-seriously.

"Oh, Frank, you are a card," Patricia said, licking her lips suggestively and leering.

We walked slowly to the pool. Brian sat there staring into the stagnant leaf-covered water; Jake wandered about under the diving board, keeping a wary eye on everything.

"Is this rude?" I asked. "Walking away, rather than toward the prince of darkness and his entourage?"

"Sensitive souls not being sensitive," Patricia said. "But they simply *have* to understand."

We sat down on the pool's edge, across from Brian. He gave us a nasty look and got up to follow Jake into the gazebo. Brian squatted on a rusty iron table and stared out of the shadows like a cheap crucifix with electric eyes.

"Why, if I weren't a lady, I would throw off my pumps and dangle my feet in this scummy water," Patricia said, and then did just that. "I guess it's the artist in me."

"My dear," I asked in my best Bela Lugosi voice, "what do you see when you look into the water?" Patricia, I suspected, was clairvoyant.

"Yeah, Patricia," Frank said, sliding his hand gently over her leg, and then mine. "What do you see?"

Patricia laughed a laugh like bubbles escaping, bursting. A faint wind stirred the floating leaves; small oily waves moved across the pool toward us.

"Nothing," she said in a voice suddenly serious, and not a little afraid.

"My God, she is a seer!" I said. "She saw something—too horrible to mention!"

"Who's a seer?" Paul Marks's voice rolled down to us through the airwaves. I looked over my shoulder, tracing the source of the broadcast; he had come up on automatic feet, and stood there blocking the twilight sky.

Over his shoulder my living-room window glimmered through the rattling tree. I imagined that I leapt over him, and flew up to the window; standing there on the thin peeling windowsill, I would cast a spell on the party, putting everyone to sleep.

"Patricia is the seer," I said, giggling; the liquor had shot through my empty stomach in record time. "She used to do fortune-telling in a circus."

"Hardly, darling," Patricia said, shaking the dismay from her eyes and replacing it with a calm amusement. She's good, I thought; I bet she's a crackerjack actress. "I work in a calamari restaurant. You really should try it sometime, Paul. Squid prepared in an infinite number of tasty ways. Like spiced rubbers."

Paul's undead girlfriend aroused herself, moved effortlessly across the yard as though she had wheels. Another feminine voice encroaching on her territory. Dimly, in her brain, a dull acquisitiveness had probably taken over.

She pressed into the triangle between Paul's perfectly poised casual shoulder and artfully draped pectoralis major. She glared at me briefly. Glass eyes, pupils big as billiard balls.

Frank and I stood up obediently. "Don't think I've met the lady," Frank said.

"Ellen, I'd like you to meet Frank." They shook hands; Frank pulled out of the limp handshake rather too quickly, earning a puzzled glance from Paul. Had the sculptor failed in creating a truly seductive beauty? Was it so beautiful that it (Ellen) intimidated?

"Ellen, have you met . . . Michael is it? Yes, Michael." He's pushing it, I thought: he knows my name as well as his own.

"At the table"—she rolled her eyes mockingly—"over there."

"Over there?" Paul asked. "Always over there. Grass is greener. Let's have another drink, shall we?"

Paul led; we followed. Patricia looked at Frank; Frank looked at me uncomprehendingly. Yet we moved, as though on chains.

Before we knew it, we were all standing about the table while Paul poured us drinks. He thinks he owns the place, I thought. He moved in after me; what gives him the right?

"Well, Paul," Frank said pleasantly, "how's business?"

"Things are incredibly busy. I had to go into partnership with Dr. Marshall Long—just relocated from back East. We have three girls in the office now. The phones never stop ringing."

Ellen sipped her drink and stared at the pool. "Why

doesn't somebody clean it up?" She raised a slender immaculate finger.

"I rather like the leaves," Patricia said. "Gives the pool character. Like moles or birthmarks, distinctive, lending individuality."

Paul stared at Patricia dumbly. Ellen continued to watch the pool, as though hoping to see something; and apparently failing. She had the fractured look of someone who had just awakened from a lifetime coma.

"Patricia has the artistic head in the building—she's a honey." Frank hugged her. They clinked their glasses, and amber liquor flew.

"Whoops, one too many," Patricia giggled.

The side door opened. Janette, pink jumpsuit unzipped almost to the waist, cream-colored pearls against caramel-colored flesh, and a single silver bracelet, entered. Behind her was a stunning woman, vast amounts of shiny black hair with red highlights, and lips so full it seemed they would burst. All this seen from fifty feet. Behind Janette's companion, Fred Feretti followed at a discreet distance, like a warrior watching over his entourage.

"My God," Patricia said, "give me strength."

"Darling, how *are* you?" Janette said in the general direction of our disintegrating group. Everyone thought she meant him or her: we piped our hellos at the same time, a drunken chorus.

So, I thought, feeling amused at last, trying to suppress the smirk that was forcing itself onto my face, Janette has learned well from Paul. She has just taken the center of attention from his whirring vacuum and replaced it with a completely disarming and charming insincerity.

Michael, I said under my breath, hoping to be mistaken for the wind, get yourself under control. I swallowed the laugh, three times. Remember—appropriate behavior in public places.

"And . . ." Janette said, rushing upon us like a flash of pink lightning, "this is Margaret."

Margaret shook hands, lingering (I imagined) over mine.

She flushed, her face a pool of shadow and light, softly blending. Perhaps embarrassed by her own beauty, she radiated a benign field of innocence.

Paul looked up hungrily, his eyes taking in every motion. Here was a woman who could be a model for his other creations. He must hate her, I thought, because he didn't think her up himself.

Margaret dropped his hand quickly, and gracefully returned to Janette's side. Ellen was boring holes in Margaret with her eyes.

"Hello, Michael," Fred Feretti said, moving in for the kill. I could see he figured he wasn't going to get much from Janette tonight, so his attention, like an erection with a homing device, was moving in my direction. I remembered what Janette had told me about Dr. Feretti's attraction for me, and stood my ground, although I wanted to turn and run.

"How's the new place?" he growled. His arms were bent and blood vessels like ropes protruded along the bronze flesh.

"Not so new anymore," I said, breathing the cloud of him. He must have been loaded with testosterone; you could almost feel it in the air, a greasy intoxicating vapor.

Paul Marks watched us with eagle eyes; he had spread his legs like a soldier holding a machine gun. Being the number-one man is such a hard thing, I thought. I wondered if he had seen one movie too many. He cleared his throat, a deep bellow like a wounded animal's.

We stood about in a circle like a coven about to begin some bizarre rite.

"All right, where's the bloody liquor?" Janette said. Margaret smiled dazzlingly (poor girl, she couldn't help it). "I'll get you something," she said, and kissed Janette noisily on the lips.

Paul Marks growled again. Ellen looked nonplussed; she was a sophisticate.

"Lived in the city long, Paul?" I asked, seizing upon an opportunity to be irritating.

"For years, since I was a kid," he said. He was lying; Janette had told me he was from Sonoma, and had lived there until recently. This was his first city address.

Janette had gone over to the barbecue pit and was supervising the coals. When the smoke started to rise, Paul seemed to relax. In his own milieu at last, drunken barbecues under a lifeless sky.

"Lesbians," Patricia said, finishing off another one, "are so interesting. Not so narcissistic as gay men. No offense, Billy," she called across the yard to where Billy and his comparable companion were now talking with Margaret.

I could see the thoughts going through Paul Marks's mind as clearly as words across an advertising screen. He hated the idea of two women together, and yet hoped to have them both under his control by the end of the evening.

His eyes had grown palpably huge.

"Frank," I said, pulling him from the breaking circle, "let's go see what Brian is up to. Excuse us."

We went to the pool. "Do you swim, Frank?" I asked.

He nodded. "Sometimes. But mostly weights and running. How about you?"

"Oh, not often, but I think when it warms up and the filter is turned on, I might try it."

As I looked into the cool oily water, the idea seemed unlikely, though somehow attractive.

Smoke now poured into the sky. It seemed to hover over the increasingly boisterous gathering like a dark cloud that would never release its rain.

"This winter," I said. "It's been months since it's rained. I feel just like the sky—dry and used up. Know what I mean?"

"Know, how can you ask that when . . . ?" Frank pointed to the end of the pool where Brian was sitting on Jake's back.

Janette screamed. I looked up. She was holding her hand. Margaret had rushed to her side. "Goddammit," she shouted, "burned myself. Margaret, you shouldn't let me drink so much."

Fred Feretti stood across from Paul Marks; identical poses, they mirrored each other. Oh, boy, I thought, we're going to have a dogfight.

"Get that," I said to Frank, and pointed.

"Human nature," he said. "What can you do about it?"

"Oh, Frank, be serious," I said, and rubbed my hand up his thigh, as a joke.

Brian rushed over.

"Dad, Mom said I shouldn't be up so late. I want to go to bed." Brian glared at me.

"Okay. Be right back down, Michael." And then he was off, fading through the crowd back into the empty building.

"Billy," I said flirtatiously, "do you know how good-looking you are?"

He laughed charmingly, looked at his knees, which he had suddenly pulled together. "I have my good and bad days," he said finally.

Billy's friend had joined us; he looked like a paler version of Billy, same body, same tilt of head, same hair, like a reflection seen in a sun-flooded mirror.

I felt suddenly angry. Billy's friend, sitting on the arm of the lawn chair, put his arm around Billy.

Okay, Michael, I murmured; let's figure this out. I tried to relax my clenching mind, but everything went behind my eyes and locked the two handsome young men in a hard gaze. The more I looked, the less I saw. My face felt like one big knot of tension.

Suddenly I wanted my mirror. I had drunk too much. Maybe I was mad at Billy because he had what I wanted: someone in his own image, someone real.

I excused myself, got another drink. The drink burned, but when it hit my stomach, the tension released in one quick burst.

I stared at myself in the cut glass. A dozen images, looking scary and scared. Eyes as cold as marbles.

Not me at all.

* * *

"My head is woozy," Patricia said, after we had eaten. Janette sat in the lawn chair, staring at her bandaged hand.

"Can you believe it?" she said. "When I was little I used to wear bandages to get sympathy."

"How's it feel?" I asked.

"Numb. Paul had some anesthetic ointment." She ran her undamaged hand through her hair. "I hate these affairs. Bloody boring, and something always happens. I am such a damned klutz."

"Don't be so hard on yourself," Patricia said blurrily. "You still look great. Look at me." She leaned forward and stared into the silver-and-black water. "That is the face of a rumpled drunken woman."

"But very fetching," I said. "You need some aspirin?"

"You mean go upstairs and miss the finale? Not on your life. I never leave until a play is over."

Janette looked startled. "Patricia, that edge of cynicism is new for you. Where'd you pick it up?"

Patricia laughed. "Don't know. Free-floating, ran into a cloud of it a while back, and got poisoned."

Janette nodded tiredly. "I'm sure my hand is throbbing, though I can't feel it. Subliminal. Makes you irritable. Speaking of which, Michael, you've suddenly gotten quiet. Is there some deep dark secret you're hiding?" Janette said. She turned pale. "Oops, didn't mean to offend."

Patricia looked perplexed, but said nothing. I nodded raggedly, pretending to be drunker than I was.

There were small dark groups of people all over the yard, like congealing blood. I kept my eyes unfocused so I could not distinguish faces. Make them clouds, I thought, and maybe they will float away. The air was dry, silent, with a faint undertone of ozone and insecticide.

I looked for stars, but the city lights reflecting from the dome of unmoving air hid them.

"Rain, rain, rain," Patricia said in a singsong voice, "a little rain would clear the air and bring this party to a merciful end."

Paul came up behind us. The clock started to tick again. Everything was suddenly *all* faces.

"Michael," he said in that low, low voice, "I just saw someone standing up in your window. It looked just like you."

A little later Janette said, distantly, her eyes half-caught in some private rumination, "Maybe you should go up and check. Could be a burglar. Everyone down here is so loaded, someone might have climbed up the side of the building and gotten in."

"Paul was being dramatic. He can't stand it when people relax. He doesn't get enough attention from a relaxed mind."

"Still, you'd better see. I talked to the guy next door, middle floor, rear, a few days ago and he said someone climbed into his place when he was gone, and shit in the middle of his bed."

"Ugh, Janette!" Patricia said, rolling her eyes heavenward. "You're not serious."

"All too serious. And it's not uncommon at all—apparently burglars are dogs at heart."

"Okay, I'll check," I said, getting up on numb legs. "Tell Frank when he comes back down that I've gone up for a while. If I don't fall asleep or get killed, then I'll probably be back down."

"Where is Frank anyway?" Patricia asked.

"Checking on Brian."

"For the third time? Why doesn't he give them both a break and let the kid alone?" Patricia said.

"Product of an overly disciplined childhood, my lady?" I asked as I disappeared under the shadow of the balcony.

"Well, you can't replace love with discipline, or with a sense of responsibility, that's for certain," Patricia said.

Patricia sounded strident; I smiled. Liquor had brought out her impatient hidden face.

The back stairs smelled like flea powder and garbage. There was a radio on in an upper apartment, and low garbled voices. Someone had quit the party early. I had lost head count long ago.

I fumbled the key into the back door bolt and pushed my way in.

I felt a brief moment of disorientation. I thought maybe I had gotten into the wrong apartment. But no, there was my windbreaker thrown over the kitchen chair, the dying plant over the sink, my house slippers lying in the doorway to the living room.

Yet I moved slowly, cautiously, padding as a burglar might. The air was full, heavy, like charged air before a storm hits.

I remembered reading the Question Man in the paper the other day. "How many times do you look in the mirror each day?" Two, three, six times (the latter person admitted embarrassedly). The liars. There was no way to avoid your reflection; there were shiny surfaces everywhere. And few people could resist themselves.

I ran fingers through damp hair. I must look awful. Better check myself out.

As I entered the bedroom, something jumped out from under the bed, dark and fast.

I struggled with it and fell to the floor as its teeth found my throat.

17

"**W**ell, this has been a night to remember," Patricia said.

Patricia was on one side of me, Frank on the other.

"Do you think you feel strong enough to leave?" Frank asked, his eyes wild with concern. A stiff-lipped nurse looked at me suspiciously.

I knew what she was thinking: What kind of a man is it whose own dog turns on him?

Patricia gave the nurse a dirty look as she and Frank lifted me from the chartreuse chair. "Thanks *so* much for all your help," Patricia said. The emergency-room people had kept me waiting for twenty minutes while I bled into the towel they had provided.

I noted with dismay, as the automatic doors opened, that the bloody towel was still sitting next to the sand-filled ashcan.

"Does it hurt?" Frank asked. He tightened his arm around my shoulders.

"What?" I said, trying to sound funny and incredulous; I did not feel funny. I had to go home and face a difficult decision. "Your steely grip, or my stitches?" Three stitches in my neck, two in my upper arm.

"I wonder if Jake got into somebody's drugs?" Patricia asked. "Once a kitten I was sitting for ate a lid of dope, went through some interesting and—I hate to admit it—

amusing antics, then died in convulsions. Maybe Jake ate some cocaine. I can't imagine marijuana would turn him psychotic."

I had swallowed two Tylenol #3 tablets. It was the full moon. The moonlight seemed to unscrew the top of my head and send me flying. I could feel my weight diminish, my self spreading thin on the wind. Not altogether an unpleasant sensation.

"What are you going to do about Jake?" Frank asked. Jake was now locked in the laundry room.

"Don't know, don't know," I answered blearily. "Maybe he thought I was a burglar. When he jumped at me he looked at me like that—as though he had never seen me before. He's never been completely there, you know. But I love him."

My voice sounded tinny, inconsequential.

There was something unnerving about a well-lit night.

"Well, no matter what, is he going to be safe to have around now? Will you ever trust him again?" Patricia's voice was pained.

"Umm—" I moaned like a brain-damage case. Was I drooling too?

"Michael, are you sure you're all right?" Patricia asked. "You seem so far away all of a sudden ..."

"Quiet, Patricia." Frank said. "That's how he handles things. I'm like that too. Right, buddy?"

I nodded weakly, walking under the pouring moon. We found the car in the silver parking lot and got in.

"Well, I never ..." Patricia said, not really dismayed. "You men. Strong, silent brothers. Me didn't mean to trespass."

"Oh, Pat ..." Frank said (we never called her Pat), "you know I didn't mean to leave you out."

"Forget it," Patricia said, now becoming slightly edgy. "Drive."

The car stopped at a red light; a man in an oversize canvas outfit like a tent huffed and puffed by, his eyes ablaze. He slowed down; he looked at my bandages, then into my starry eyes. The light changed. Frank stepped on the gas, and slowly moved around the man, who blocked the fender and didn't look like he was going to move. The fender brushed the man as we pulled slowly away. No harm done, but a definite touch.

The man shot to the other side of the street, as though struck by lightning.

"Let's get out of here before we're in the middle of a lawsuit," Frank said.

When we were almost home, a car pulled alongside us, gunned its motor, then cut in front of us. Frank had to slam on the brakes to avoid hitting the car. I was thrown forward; Patricia, who wore her seat belt, grabbed me just before my head hit the glass.

"Goddammit, they're after us tonight," Frank said.

I looked at the car, which had stopped in front of a Ma and Pa store. Frank shouted, "Hey, you idiots, what's the big rush?"

The door opened. There were four nuns in the car.

"If you want to stay home tomorrow night," Patricia said in front of my door, "it's okay. We can go out another time."

"I don't know. Maybe it would do me good to get out. It doesn't seem like huddling inside is safe anymore, if you know what I mean."

"It's up to you. And if you need any help with Jake, let me know. Otherwise, I'll see you tomorrow." Patricia seemed suddenly shy. She leaned forward, her milky skin paler than usual, her eyes unwilling to meet mine.

I suspected she intended to kiss me on the cheek. But her mouth landed on my mouth, just as I was about to say good night, and her lips met my tongue.

She put her arms around me. My heart flew into my throat.

I thought of the times I had climbed upon the balcony and spied on Paul Marks sitting in front of a video screen watching pornography, his legs spread, sometimes with a woman, sometimes alone, but always with the same intent vacancy.

"Thanks for everything tonight," I said. "Without you and Frank I don't think I could have gotten through this." Formal but true. I kept my arms around her but didn't pursue the embrace.

"Okay, that's okay," Patricia said, disentangling herself. "I'll fill Janette and the others in on what happened, if they're still up. *You* go to bed."

I hesitated at the door. I was afraid of being out here with Patricia.

But I was equally afraid to go inside.

I slept deeply, dreamlessly, and woke oddly refreshed. The stitches had begun to ache. I lingered over breakfast, drank a pot of coffee, read the paper from front to back. Anything to avoid going downstairs and seeing Jake.

I would be late for work if I stalled any longer. Pulling on my gray coat, I went down the back stairs to the laundry room.

Patricia stood outside the darkened room. The door was open. For a moment I stopped, shook, waited. Then descended.

"What's wrong?" I cried, grabbing her hand. Her face was dry and pinched, her eyes glittering with tears.

"It's Jake," Patricia sobbed. "He's dead. His neck is broken."

"Are you sure you can drive?" Patricia asked.

"Sure, I'm all right. My neck hurts a little bit, but my arm feels fine. Really. Like nothing happened."

"Well, I'm not so sure. How can you want to go out after all this? Men! I would be a basket case if I were you. I am a basket case, and I'm not you!" She laughed nervously. "And now we have a mystery to solve."

"Mystery? Oh, you mean . . . well, two actually. Why Jake attacked me, and how he died." I felt suddenly logical. "The man from the SPCA said he could have eaten something foreign, attacked me in his confusion—animals will do that when they're afraid—then, after I'd locked him up, had a convulsion, banged his head against something so hard that he snapped his neck. Or jumped up on the washer, had a convulsion, and fell off, breaking his neck. What mystery?"

"Well, if you are consoled by thinking that, then go right ahead. Me, I'm very uneasy about the whole thing. I dreamt last night like a fiend, but couldn't remember any of it, which isn't like me." Patricia had tied her hair up casually, as though she were about to shower; she wore a black lace dress with a flaring skirt, and silver shoes. I wore a black double-breasted suit with baggy pants, and leather bedroom slippers with no socks (the slippers had belonged to my dad).

Patricia had forgotten the exact location of the club; we wound through blind empty alleys for a half-hour, searching.

"There it is!" Patricia said, just missing my nose with her pointing finger.

"Where what is?" I looked down the trajectory of her finger, but saw only darkness, a squat gray building, a semi-open door. Then movement identified itself, a slithering out of the antiseptic alley dark, in this gentrified warehouse district. People in line, silent, no smoke, no fire; if you didn't look hard, you'd have missed them entirely.

"My God, I've got to stand in that," I moaned. "More of the same." Patricia leaned against my shoulder.

"Looks pretty grim, doesn't it, sort of like the spawn of Paul Marks, only with more hair spray. But I know the guy who runs the door—remember I told you?—so we can avoid the standing-and-waiting part, at least."

"Oh, yeah, we may enjoy the privilege of stepping in front of ... of those ..."

"Young moderns. With a few postmoderns mixed in. Those are the ones trying to talk and move. Forward and back, side to side. Little lost lambs in search of another fashion."

We found a parking spot just around the corner; the street was deserted, no people, no cars. Where had the people in the line come from? There was no one on foot, and no public transportation. Had they beamed down from above?

Turning the corner, through the dank air, I waited for something to give me an indication. A raised voice, a honking horn. Not even the faint fishy smell of the sea.

"Michael, you're holding up really well. Maybe if we dance till we drop, you'll get your anxiety out. But I'm afraid when you wake up tomorrow, today is going to land on your head like a ton of bricks."

We wound our way through the silent glassy-eyed patrons. A couple of people turned toward us with casual eye movements. I thought: Their eyes are moving outside their bodies. I was reminded of waxy white eggs caught in nets of gelatin.

Patricia leaned over the rope, whispered something in the ear of the surprisingly normal-looking doorman; dressed in jeans and white T-shirt, he looked incongruous; yet he was the man to contend with, the judge of the fashion show.

"Pat," he cried, leaning forward with an expression of unabashed pleasure. "How nice to see you. It's been—"

"Let's not talk about how long it's been. And let's not make it any longer. Get us inside, and I'll write down my new phone number. We'll have lunch—in a day or two. I mean it—in a day or two."

He escorted us in. The people in line gave us the fish eye. I could feel it crawling up my spine, like radiation. I wondered who they thought we were.

We checked our coats with a rosy-faced girl who looked like she should be singing at a Miss America contest, wound our way down uncarpeted concrete stairs, then up some more stairs, into a low-ceilinged room with a silver ball scattering sperm-shaped bits of light over the dancers.

"Boy, you'd think they'd have come up with something new," I said to Patricia.

"Something new? Don't be ridiculous. They should have called this placed Echoes."

"Patricia, Janette was right. Deep down, you are a cynic. I always thought you were an idealist."

"Same thing," she shouted in my ear. A deafening industrial dance number had come on.

We moved into a small alcove where it was a little quieter. I kept my eyes glued to Patricia, not yet ready to face the crowd.

"Funny thing," Patricia said, "there used to be real factories in this area, making all kinds of noise. I lived in a loft about two blocks from here. Now they've moved the factories to Oakland or down the peninsula, but they play music that tries to recreate that past. You will find no pitons here, no grease, just—"

A pale-faced young man walked by; the front of his hair stood out in an eight-inch spike. He swiveled past me, and the spike grazed my cheek.

I shoved him aside, reflexively. He lurched like a shot rabbit, spilling his drink. He looked smug, then like he was going to cry, then disinterested again. An overweight girl dressed in black (clothes, eyes, hair, lipstick, fingernails) gave me a dirty look.

"Not a very scary lot, are they?"

"No, they don't take their gothic seriously enough."

Patricia suggested we dance. I said I'd have to wait for something a little more melodic.

"This may be a long wait. Let's mingle." She grabbed my arm and we were off.

I looked around the room, at the clustered bobbing

heads. We dived in. From one side to the other, and nothing stuck. And back again.

"Is this the work ethic gone mad?"I asked. "I feel like I've just spent eight hours at a typewriter."

The place was jammed. I watched from a dark corner. People would artfully dodge each other, though there was scarely an inch or two between. Such avoidance was a talent. On those rare ocassions when clothing touched, there was a silent sliding away, catlike.

"Let's go upstairs," Patricia suggested after we had fortified ourselves with two kamikazies each. "Much ado about nothing."

"Patricia, you know, if I didn't have you, I don't think ... well, I don't think ..." I said, my heart getting sloppy with alcohol.

"Please, dear, this is not the time or place. But thanks. Ditto."

Upstairs was the video room. There were dozens of round tables, small uncomfortable wooden chairs. There was not an empty chair in the house. On the two video screens a man with red spots all over him was running, sweating, through a shimmering cellophane urban nightmare. The music pounded, the people stared.

"No talking allowed," Patricia said, chortling. She tumbled through the chairs, charmingly excusing herself when she stepped on toes, winding her way to the two seats that had just been vacated.

"Here, sit. You look like you need to. It's not payment time, is it?"

"Huh? Oh, no, I just seem to be absorbing something here, a kind of bad dream in which nothing happens, one of those endless-door dreams, you know the one."

"Oh, my, you are having a good time," Patricia said. She grabbed the barmaid, a suburban-dour girl in a dog collar. "Two kamikazies—and hurry."

The video changed. Sand dunes, long sinuous camera angles moving up and over, suggestively, like an eye traveling up the terrain of a body. Blurry euphoric music, almost romantic.

Shake me; I must be dreaming.

The camera zoomed in on a face; the desert had been a body after all.

"Oops, drinks didn't get here soon enough," Patricia said.

The face on the screens was Dr. Paul Marks's.

"How d'you suppose he got himself involved in this sort of scene? He's a doctor, not a model."

"Oh, Michael, really," Patricia said. "Think of what kind of doctor he is. This is an appropriate homage."

The video continued. The tempo of the music had become insinuating, like a distant piston banging, like an imbecilic foot thumping.

Like the feet of Paul Marks's bed as he pinned his victims noisily to the mattress, thinking of what alterations he might perform.

"Well, I think we give him entirely too much attention. But then, you know, I noticed at the barbecue the other night that he does have a strange sort of attraction, even for me, and I don't like the man. But he has a power, an *influence.*" Patricia looked thoughtful, perplexed, then continued. "He may be history in the making."

"Weird. Even you. Patricia, I thought you of all people would be immune." My words slurred, dripped; I was half-drunk already. From the momentum, I could tell that in an hour I'd be completely gone.

"No one's immune. We only think we are, that we're special or different. In a way I guess Paul represents a painful truth."

The face, those eyes, now shifting in a psychedelic pattern, eye becoming mouth, mouth swelling to fill the screen, teeth as shiny and bright as scalpels.

We were sitting near the front, right under the radiating screens. I turned around to gauge the audience reaction to my neighbor's melting visage. Hair, fixated eyes, no movement.

"Michael, don't take it so seriously. I shouldn't have brought you here. You have that high tragic look."

She put her arm around me. I nuzzled into her shoulder, drunkenly. She lifted me up; my body felt lighter than air, my head dangled, as though half-severed.

"Mommy," I slobbered.

"Let's get out of here." Patricia led me expertly through the masses. "Excuse us, he's going to be sick." The way was instantly, silently made for our passage out.

"Loved the videos," Patricia said drolly to the doorman as we passed out the front door; there was a line a half-block long waiting to get in.

"They'll never make it," I said.

I was collapsed in the passenger seat. "You have to drive, I'm a wreck," I said. Patricia was leaning against me heavily, sensuously.

Before I knew what I was doing, I was kissing her. I ran my hands over her face, flicked my tongue over her eyelids, which fluttered like racing hearts. I cupped her head in my hands and looked at her dusky eyes, the fine bones of her face, her nose, the full but humorous lips.

I started to slip my hand under her blouse, but she stopped me. "Michael, if we're going to make love, let's go home."

I looked up; two anesthetized creatures from the club had come round the corner and were peering blankly into the car.

"Okay," I said. "You drive." I knew the moment was lost once the engine started.

I grew more uncomfortable on the way home. The car seemed too small, the sky too close. When we got there I said, "Patricia, I feel strange. I'm going to go for a drive by myself, maybe get some coffee. Okay?"

"Are you sure?" she said, searching my eyes. She looked disappointed but resigned. "You seemed to have sobered up suddenly."

I walked her to her front door, stopped at my place to

pick up my gym bag. Maybe I'd go to the twenty-four-hour Nautilus and work off some of this angst.

Then I was reeling into the night.

All was silent but for the hissing of the tires and the pounding of my blood.

18

I drove carefully. Police were everywhere. I hoped I was not driving too carefully. Drunk people always did that. Cops were trained to know.

At first I just wandered. Then I passed both apartments where Dorothy and I had lived.

I wanted to get away, from Patricia, the building, my home, myself.

This was not the way.

I crept up on the crosswalks, gauging foot pressure through my foggy mind. I was not sober; far from it. It was an act, an elaborate deception, this apparent sobriety. A couple of cars honked at me. "Old lady," someone shouted.

I picked up the pace a little, took several corners rather wide, almost ended up on the subdivider, next to a palm tree.

The scraping of my fender on the concrete curb jarred something loose.

I did a quick U-turn and headed downtown. A little place I knew, where the people were hungry and showed it. I was hungry too, for something other than myself.

I found a parking spot right in front of The Blue Man, spelled out in neon next to a cocktail glass whose lights were burnt out.

As I stepped out of the car, I wondered how I had gotten across town. I was simply *here,* at my destination, after having formulated the thought. There was no between, no connective tissue.

The air smelled greasy, hot. There were hookers standing in the doorways, transvestites prowling about, a midget with long stringy hair smoking a cigar; garbage in the gutters, like rotting flowers.

I wobbled across the street.

"Hey, honey, had a little bit too much?" came a falsetto voice from a dark doorway. "How'd you like a little more? Twenty bucks, best blow-job in the City."

There were snickers, a chorus of them, merging with hissing tires, sizzling neon, steam rising through the streets. "Best blow-job, my ass," someone countered, a real woman's voice, I thought. "Try this!" And I heard the snap of elastic, then the click click click of high heels coming my way.

I ducked inside the bar. The doorman's seat was empty; I pressed through the tattered leather curtain into the sweaty, musty-smelling interior. Blue light, a badly scarred pool table, a polished teak bar reflecting the flickering fluorescent lights that gave the place its ghastly pallor.

The bar was empty. Two overweight creatures of interderminate sex hovered over the pool table, under a chipped white hanging light. Cigarette smoke twisted about their heads.

I ordered a drink; the bartender looked at me oddly, but brought the drink and took my money.

He was not the sort of bartender you unburden yourself to. No wisdom here, no solace.

I sipped the drink slowly, savoring the burning line from mouth to stomach. Suddenly I was on fire all over, like a brushfire encouraged by an insistent wind.

"Hey, are you all right?" the bartender asked cursorily.

I was having double vision; I had four hands. When I looked at my face reflected in the bartop, I had four eyes.

A wind whispered behind me, a cloud of perfume, a soft gentle pressure.

I turned around slowly.

"Hello." Deep voice, natural. Almost masculine. Dark

hair, pale skin, fine features. Black dress, low-cut, with a single white flower nestled between ample breasts. She smelled like sweat and perfume and city night air.

"Hello," I said, looking her over. "Please . . . sit down." I patted the cracked Leatherette stool.

Bar talk, at first. Do you come here often, do you live in the city; I was so loaded it almost sounded sincere. Then something about her mother, who had just died, or was about to die. I didn't pay much attention, but replied appropriately, my eyes pinned to her breasts, wondering what they would taste like, later.

She noticed my attention, and talked more. Words flooded from her. She was excited, her face flushed. Then she put a slender white hand over mine, running a finger up and down the veins in my forearm.

"Do you have someplace we could go?" I asked at what seemed the right moment.

"Oh . . ." she said, apparently taken aback (I guessed a feeble attempt at cat and mouse). "I guess we could . . ." Then she paused, looking me deeply in the eyes. My eyes felt cold, but I tried to pump some warmth into them.

"I mean, it's smelly in here, and close. Maybe we would be more comfortable . . . somewhere else."

This seemed to satisfy her, though the meaning was the same: where could we go and have a quick fuck? Not my place, for a number of unspoken reasons. Protocol. You have to phrase these things delicately, lie with finesse.

I put my arm around her waist, surprised that it was not as slender as it appeared.

Under the streetlights, what I had taken to be a fair complexion was pale powder that caked a little about her mouth. Her eyes were dark, yet the eye liner was thick, and her eyes, vaguely red, were watery.

Like a caricature of Patricia. Same type, wrong person. Yet there was a worn sweetness about her that kept me from making that final excuse and darting back to my car.

"I live just around the corner," she said breathlessly. We walked fast. The street was now quiet, the doorways empty.

"Moody," I said, feeling tired. "This city is so moody. One minute the streets are full of people, the next they are empty. And you can never tell why. Never."

I felt like I was about to blow apart. An erection scratched against my pants. We entered a nondescript five-story building. Up the tattered Oriental runner, one story, then two. Smell of dust and grease and mold. My erection got harder. I had to pee. That sensation increased my pleasure. I would hold it until I was about to burst.

And then let it explode.

Her apartment was small and demonstrated a genteel poverty. Flowered prints everywhere; the smell of perfume that she emanated in the bar was overpowering here.

A folding bed, which she abruptly pulled out from the wall.

"More comfortable than the couch," she said shyly. I smiled.

The bathroom was visible from the couch. She had brought out two paper cups of wine. I reached over and slowly removed the flower from between her breasts.

She sighed, then pressed her damp cleavage against my palm.

Suddenly the pressure in my groin was too much. "Can I use the bathroom first?" I asked.

The bathroom mirror called, sirenlike. I dared not disobey.

While I pissed, relishing the sudden warm rush, I stared into the mirror, cracked, worn, with whorls of degenerating silver that looked like thumbprints.

I leaned my head against the surface while zipping up. The cold surface seemed to sober me. I pushed forward, wanting more.

There was a slight tug, as if something were trying to draw me back into the real world, then the surface of the mirror released, and I fell through, headfirst, like tumbling through a window—first a giddy free-fall, then a soft affectless landing.

I stood up, dusted my knees, and looked out. There was the not-so-young woman sitting patiently on the greasy green bed, waiting.

There was the young man leaning against the mirror. I met his eyes. Not mine. I reached to the glass, but could not get back through.

He turned and walked away from me into the other room.

Helpless, trapped in the mirror world, I could only watch.

The man's hair was dark, darker than mine, although my hair was growing darker by the day. He now wore a mask of some kind; at first I could not see it clearly. It was as though he were teasing me, keeping his back to me.

When he finally turned, I saw that the mask was metal, with shiny razors for eyes, with a nose like a steel spike, lips like sharp flowers.

The woman on the couch looked at him with disbelief. The man's tongue lashed out lizardlike through the narrow mouth hole.

"No," she said, crawling into the pillows, "I won't kiss you with that on.

He peeled the mask off, revealing another underneath. This one was of burnished metal, not as reflective, and the edges were softer. Yet I could see that it was dangerous still; the edges were blunted, but would cut, only with more subtlety.

"No," the woman said with surprising control. This was clearly not her first strange encounter. "Not that one either."

Underneath that mask was another mask, made of shiny cloth; it shimmered like pearls, like sea foam. I felt the allure even where I stood.

The man leaned down and began kissing the woman. She responded feverishly, pressing her lips to the cloth. The lovemaking grew in intensity; the cloth mask was pushed aside from time to time. Beneath was another mask (or the real face?) of the man. It was smooth, bright like a mirror, and featureless.

She slid out of her blouse. Her breasts were heavy, blue-veined.

She reached for the man's zipper. He backed away, removing his belt and dropping his pants in a single motion. His penis was so engorged with blood that it quivered. A red cloth was tied around the middle.

The woman shed all her clothes. They lay on the floor like discarded feelings.

The man reached into a small gym bag next to the folding bed. He pulled out a piece of barbed wire. He wrapped it underneath the head of his penis, careful that the barbs pointed outward.

The woman looked up worriedly. He leaned down and his shadow covered her. I saw only her struggling legs. He raised up suddenly, for she was pushing him away with legs, with arms; no, he could not enter her that way.

He moved aside. The woman now wore the mask. She lay there waiting, legs parted, still but for her panting breath.

The man removed the knife from the bag and placed it on the moist groin of the masked woman.

I pounded my fists against the glass, but the sound rolled back upon me in silent waves.

Impotent, sickened, I closed my eyes.

And heard the swift motion of the blade.

19

I dreamed I didn't exist.
When I woke the next morning, I found that I didn't.

There was a knock at the door, punching a hole in the wall of sleep. I crawled through.

Standing in the open front door, I blinked into the light. Fluorescent fixture, like a halo, behind her head.

"Jesus, you need coffee, and now." Patricia pushed past my corpse, made rustling sounds in the kitchen.

I, or whatever it was that had been retrieved from sleep and the endeavors of the night before, moved on stiff limbs to the couch, sat on the sun-warmed fabric.

Soon the smell of coffee reached me, made me remember what it was like to be human.

"I know I should be mad at you," Patricia said, putting the coffee on a blue coaster, "but I guess you were just afraid. Fear is something that I understand all too well."

I held the cup, hoarding the warmth.

"Maybe you shouldn't understand it so well," I said. "You can get infected by it. Better to hate fear."

"Whatever you say. Keep drinking that coffee." She paused. "Have you looked in the mirror this morning?"

I couldn't tell her that I had spent the night *in* the mirror. "No, I haven't," I said lamely. "Pretty bad, huh?"

"Pretty bad is right. Your face is creased all over, like a shirt from a suitcase. And your hair—either dirty, or you get a dye job last night while you prowled the city. Did you meet a lonely hairdresser and go home with him ... with her? Any hidden tattoos?"

I stumbled to my feet, pulled up the black paper blinds; the sun poured onto my damp bed. The sheet and comforter were knotted up.

In the window glass the man who stared back at me had a face like Frankenstein's; a jigsaw face, framed with greasy locks of dark—almost black—hair.

Patricia came up behind me. She put her hand on my shoulder. "I've heard of people's hair going white from fright, but never this."

I touched my hair. It was faintly sticky, matted together.

"Ugh," I said, feeling the warm rush from the coffee; movement now seemed not only possible but also urgent.

"I've got to shower," I said. "I'm a mess. And my stomach is on fire from all that liquor. We'll talk later."

I gently but firmly moved her to the front door and into the hall.

Janette was coming down the stairs as Patricia left; she took one look at us, then went back up, as though she had forgotten something.

She probably thought Patricia and I had spent the night together.

I shut the door.

Examining my face, I noted (as though the face belonged to someone else) the dark circles under the eyes, the dilated pupils, and the stupefied stare. Was there a look of dull satisfaction as well?

Shivering, I turned on the shower. Too cold, then too hot.

I left the shower curtain open so I could watch myself in the mirror. Rubbing my hands down my hard chest, over belly all muscle and tight skin, to the pubic bone, and then holding my balls firmly, I put my head under the water.

The dark began to wash out of my hair, flowed down my body, and swirled about my feet.

It was blood.

* * *

I was sitting by the pool. The sky was clear, pale blue. It would soon be spring.

A dry winter. No snow in the mountains. Maybe water rationing this summer. I looked into the pool, wondering when the landlord was going to clean it; I had made a few furtive attempts to keep it clear of floating leaves and such, but not recently.

As I sat there, for minutes or hours, clouds formed. I saw them first in the surface of the pool, white billows which slowly darkened.

I looked up.

A line of rain was visible just over the rooftop. Under it, I could see Paul Marks moving about in his apartment, a towel wrapped around his waist, holding his groin as he paced, as if in pain.

I wondered what kind of night he had had.

I felt confused, nauseous, volcanic. Suddenly, big hot tears were splashing down my face. My tears smelled like summer rain. It was an old memory. It never rained here in the summer; only the winters were green.

I felt my face, amazed. What could be the cause? No, don't think about it. What's the use? It never gets you anywhere. The feelings that tried to surface were painful, alien.

Knowing I was a coward, I pushed them back down, deep.

I concentrated on the sky. Clouds gathered, the rain line moved over pointed black rooftops, down the darkening slopes. Let nature be the expression.

Soon a cold straight downpour had begun, washing my upraised face clear.

And the tears that I supposed had been my own were no longer tears.

I read the paper, drank two pots of coffee, staring out the window at the pelting rain. In a week it would officially be spring. I had expected rain during the winter; this late rain was disturbing.

I listened to the hypnotic footsteps of Paul Marks, imagining his sinuous movements, the muscles under skin so fine and clear that it seemed not to have pores.

A caged animal in a perfect cage. Not the sort of man to like melancholy weather. Somehow, the thought comforted me. I felt an odd sympathy for him; therefore, less alone. I relaxed a bit.

Then fell asleep.

I woke headachy, my muscles stiff, as though I had been vigorously exercising while asleep. My bed was drenched. Blearily I got up and removed the sheets; the mattress pad was yellow from many nights of wet sleep.

The fresh linen smelled clean, sharp. I made the bed, letting the smell enter me, stirring up things. I took a deep breath and sat down.

And started to remember.

The street was tree-lined, dark and shaded, dead-ending in a playground. On the jungle gym in the middle of that electric green field was where, hanging like monkeys, my best friend and I had first tried out swear words.

"Fuck you, Michael, goddammit, you prick!" he said, his T-shirt riding up and showing his quarter-size navel; he was hanging barely two feet from me. My hands had started to hurt, but I couldn't let go first.

"Goddammit," he repeated when I didn't respond. I flinched; "goddammit" was a word I couldn't get used to. He knew that, and used the word a lot. His stomach somehow got bigger each time he said it. To me, the word was a breach of faith, and no fun at all.

"God damn you too," I said weakly, kicking in the air to distract my aching hands from the pain.

I swung past him, to the other side, stepped up on a ladder, and sat down, glowering. Some children played on the other side of the field, out of hearing.

Larry let go suddenly, tumbling into the sand; a painful landing. Dust rose and choked me on my perch.

"You okay?" I coughed.

"Sure," he said gruffly. "Let's go home."

I climbed down cautiously; I had ripped my head open on a protruding screw on the jungle gym at school the year before.

"Hey, look at this!" and I had climbed up on the top bar with my knees and somersaulted forward. My head grazed something, but the dizzying speed of the somersault dulled the feeling. As I woozily climbed down, the warm rush of blood covered my neck and shoulders, drained onto my chest. The other children pointed and screamed.

Larry and I put our arms around each other and exited the playground. An old lady in a housedress looked at us harshly, as she was pruning dark purple roses.

"Wonder if she heard us?" Larry asked.

"No," I said, "I think it's something else." Mother had told me that it wasn't proper for two boys our age (we were ten) to walk with their arms around each other, though it was all right for girls.

"Why not all right?" I asked.

"Just isn't. Take my word for it." Mother's voice was strained, and she finished cutting the carrots; slice slice slice, each precise movement a word I could not hear or understand.

Larry and I stood in front of my house awhile and talked. My house was a little larger than Larry's, though not much. Aluminum windows, pale green siding, rosebushes on the right side, where I sometimes found praying mantises, a shared driveway on the other, oil-stained gravel.

"Call you later," I said. Larry hurried off; he was an hour late already.

I went inside. Inside smelled like cabbage, stale air. Mom was moving about in the kitchen. She was always in the kitchen now.

Dad had died two months before.

"It's about time," she called. "Where you been?"

"With Larry."

"I know who you've been with. I asked where."

I didn't want to tell her; mothers read minds, have X-ray vision. Nothing was safe. "Oh, over there." I pointed, though she couldn't see (I pointed at a wall).

"What?" she said sharply.

"The playground. The jungle gym. Over there."

There were just the two of us. My brothers had already gone off to the Army.

We ate in silence.

I stared out the back window at the pool Dad had built in the backyard. It was almost as big as the yard, which had a redwood fence around it.

The pool was empty now.

"Mom," I said while she was knitting with ferocious concentration, "why don't we fill the pool again?"

She raised her head slowly, a cold light in her eyes. "No, never. I'm going to have it filled in with dirt as soon as I can afford it. When I get the insurance money."

"I didn't mean with dirt," I said morosely. She ignored me, having returned to a complicated stitch.

I lay in bed later, staring at the ceiling. The room was empty, the house was screamingly empty. I wanted to call Larry, but he was probably in bed. We had talked on the phone twice already, anyway. I didn't want my phone privileges taken away again, so I stayed still and tried to think about something else.

My eyes burned, my head felt dry and dead inside. Finally I fell asleep.

I woke up standing at the back door. Mom's hand was on my shoulder.

"Where do you think you're going?" she asked.

She had caught me sleepwalking again, trying to get out of the house.

I couldn't answer her. My feet were still sunk in dream. I tried to move my mouth. The effort was an agony, so I stopped trying.

Mom walked me back to my room. She shook my shoulders; she finally got a glass of water and threw it in my face.

"Wake up," she pleaded.

She kept trying, kept talking, for almost an hour she later told me. Finally I woke up; the two parts of me slammed together, hard.

I fell forward, crying, into her arms.

"What's wrong?" she said desperately, holding my shaking body to her fragrant breast. "What's wrong?"

She held me too close, too long. I pulled away, now dry-eyed, terrified.

"I'm all right," I said. I looked down at my tear-shiny hands, balled them into fists, thumbs inside. "I want to go back to sleep."

I dropped the curtain that I had draped over the mirror. I was no longer blond, by any stretch of the imagination. Who was I? Was this a test of faith?

My image today had been clever, peering out as I peered in (while holding the flap of cloth), every movement a precise mimic.

Who, I thought, who is the puppet? Who, then, is responsible?

I remembered the other night, the woman who looked like Patricia, the alcoholic blur, the knife, and then— nothing. I didn't even remember driving home.

The knife lay on the bedstand, where it had been returned. The blade was clean, polished. I bent down to examine it. A symbol, an appliance, lacking meaning without the hand of man. I could not imagine this as an instrument of violence. Something you boned chickens with, cursing that it was not sharp enough, then cutting your finger to prove you were wrong.

I lay in bed eating potato chips and watching a talk show. I kept the sound turned down low so I wouldn't disturb anyone.

There was the screeching of tires out back. Then the door from the alley burst open and slammed shut. My walls shook. Whoever was playing, was playing it for the benefit of the whole neighborhood.

I tried not to respond.

Under my window, a man's drunken voice rose, then a woman's voice on the tail of his. I recognized them immediately; and with the recognition, dread. Once this started, it could go on all night. Was it drugs, misfiring brain cells, heredity, evil?

She was Japanese, small, inscrutable; he must have been six-foot-five, an auto mechanic who worked on cars in the alley.

The voices rose to a dangerous level, the man now bellowing incoherently; the words dissolved in a fog of emotion. Grudgingly I got up and looked out the window.

The tall man had his girlfriend by her long black hair and was dragging her through shimmering rain puddles. She seemed oddly limp, her face a pale blue moon, her mouth forming a blank O. I had seen pictures of war-torn Oriental women who looked like this.

I opened the window; the window upstairs opened.

Before I could say anything, which I was considering doing, Paul Marks called out, "Hey, you, leave her alone." Radio voice from above, more authority than mine.

The assailant looked up, startled that a member of his audience had identified himself, which gave the girl the moment she needed to slip away. But she ran to a side door and into their apartment. The man, now stooped over and looking downtrodden, slouched after her, key in hand.

Through an open window in the building next door, two Latin women stared out through the pelting rain.

"Did you see that?" one said to her friend. "She didn't even cry out. And he was hurting her—bad."

I shut my window, wondering what was going to happen behind closed doors. Decided it was none of my business, and put on my raincoat.

As I locked my door, the door opened on the landing above; before I could duck down the stairs or back inside, Paul rushed down the stairs two at a time.

He was wearing pale blue boxer shorts and a gold chain about his strong neck.

"Hey, Michael," he said, "some scene outside, huh?" He gave me a hard quizzical look.

His posture was so perfect, even at this late hour, every hair in place, that he seemed almost charming. Part of his plot, his influence? I didn't know. I smiled.

He patted me affably on the shoulder. "Why don't you come up and have a drink? I'm wide-awake now—and alone."

"Okay," I said, and followed him up the stairs, still in my raincoat.

I had seen his apartment only from the outside, as I dangled from the balcony watching the endless series of women that passed through (and catching glimpses of his large collection of video pornography on the wide-screen TV).

There was a regularity about his fucking that had at first drawn my admiration, precise if a little predictable, but dull after a time. The act of watching, it seemed to me, courted the idea of surprise, of the unexpected move that would bring the vision home.

First the obligatory drink, then the "tour" of the apartment; a brief fondle, then he was on top, his hand palpating his groin, an idiosyncrasy I had not given much thought to.

I walked through his front door for the first time. Inside, it smelled like eucalyptus. Not unpleasant, but overpowering more personal smells. A dog, I thought, would be confused in this apartment. White leather couch, glass coffee table, large blue ashtray with a small mirror and a vial of white powder, bookshelves empty but for speakers and a bowling trophy.

"You bowl?" I asked as he fixed a drink at the portable bar; I could see the knotted muscles of his abdomen in the bar's mirror. He is rolling them deliberately, I thought—making a drink doesn't require much muscular effort.

"Did," he replied curtly. "When I was in high school. Along with football and other things."

He handed me the drink; cut-crystal goblet, figures of

small-headed birds with vast wings. I held the glass of dark liqueur to my face; my reflection was light above the line of the liqueur, dark below.

Sweet, heavy, surprisingly potent. I sat down, my head swimming. I remembered a killer hangover I had had on a similar drink.

"So, Michael, what do you do?" He sat down, his legs parted a little too wide, embracing an invisible horse. Blue-green veins visible through his all-year-round tan.

"I work at a hospital. Shit stuff mostly, billing forms and the like. I wanted to go into marine biology, but things got sidetracked when I married—after the divorce I never got back to it somehow."

He stared at my dully, his eyes flickering over my body. I felt I was slouching, and sat up straight. I could almost hear the voice of my father saying if you slump when you're young, you'll look like a crippled old lady when you're old.

"Yeah, I know how that is," he said. He stared at his empty glass. "Good stuff. A quick buzz."

"I feel it here." I put my hand to my stomach, which tightened as though a stranger's hand had suddenly touched it.

He laughed, modulated, precise. An impossible baritone. "A lot of women in the building. Janette, those two gay women, and Patricia." He looked at me pregnantly.

"No, nothing"—I responded to the question in his eyes—"between Patricia and me . . . nothing."

He reached for my glass; my hand reached to stop him but I ended up giving him the glass instead.

"Here, let me fill that up for you," he said.

He returned the full glass and I emptied it obediently, ignoring the warning voice in my head.

He opened the double French doors. "This is my bedroom," he said. "I guess you know that."

"Hm, yes," I said, trying to sound vague. "A good-looking guy like you must give it a workout."

"I'm surprised you haven't heard," he said, sounding disappointed. Outlined in the bedside light, he posed, as though being judged for a Mr. America contest. His shorts had fallen from a fleshless waist; I followed a bulging vein into the line of the elastic.

He pointed to a picture. I got up on wobbly legs. A square-faced young boy in a cowboy outfit, standing next to Ronald Reagan. "Taken when he was governor," Paul said proudly. "That's me, of course, in the cowboy hat."

I leaned forward to get a better look. Paul's aroma struck me; like newly unpacked stereo equipment, with a hint of cologne and lingering soap.

"Paul," I said. "I thought I was in good shape, but you're exceptional. You must really work at it." I heard myself saying this as though from a distance. No space at all between his unblemished skin and his musculature.

"I just watch what I eat, and exercise." He glanced at the bed. "Good genes, I guess."

"How are you and Janette doing, if you don't mind my asking?" I said to distract myself from giving further compliments, which seemed about to pour forth.

"She's always complaining about something—other women, or I'm not gentle enough. Shit, she's got the hardest hands of any woman I've met—like claws." He dropped his shorts. "See here, these bruises. They're from Janette."

The shorts, which hung above his pubic line, dropped the rest of the way. The shaft of his penis was bright with moisture, curving heavily, wagging slightly like a dog's tail with his imperceptible hip movement. I waited. He did not pull up his shorts, but just stood there.

Dark hair, taller than me, but not much. He moved back, beside his bed, where, down below, my mirror lay under a curtain.

"Oh, man," he said, "I'm at the mercy of my hormones sometimes." He threw his head back, the angle of his jaw was accentuated; the cleft in his chin was bone, not flesh.

I felt as though some of my substance were being sucked out. I moved, and he moved. His eyes were closed, yet he seemed expert at sensing me, reading my movements, and interpreting them with his body.

I slipped out of my clothes. I spit on my hand, staring down at my glazed erection, than at his limp penis.

I began to masturbate; the sound was wet and regular, like raindrops. He is just like me, I thought, only bigger; I am like him. He is my reflection, I am downstairs having sex with my reflection, as I often did, playing pantomime, cat and mouse.

I was hard, he was not; his flaccidity urged me on, to distinguish myself further from my image.

Suddenly I came in two muscular heaves; it landed like snow on his mildly scintillating penis.

At the touch of my come, he seemed to wake. His left hand reached to his groin, and he began to pump. He leapt from the wall, a creature from *The Twilight Zone*.

He looked over my shoulder while pushing me down on the bed, and raised my legs over my head. The penis, now erect, was even bigger up close.

"No please, no thank-you," he said, and then forced his way inside me.

"**F**rank, it's you," I said thankfully. I was still in my work clothes. I kicked off my shoes. "Come in."

He looked at me curiously. "Something going on? You look weird."

"I just got home from work," I said through my shirt. "Let me get out of this suit, and I'll feel human again."

I limped into the bedroom, one foot in my pants, one foot out.

When I came back out, in black jeans, I was still limping.

"Hurt yourself jogging?" Frank asked, sounding concerned.

"Uh, something like that."

"Boy, look at that rain coming down. Two weeks ago, dry as a bone. Now this. You'd think it could go on forever." I glanced out, no more moved than if I had been watching a film of a tropical storm.

"I've got leaks all over the place. Pans sitting on the floor, and I'm about out of dry towels. Came down to borrow some, if you can spare them. I don't suppose you have any leaks yet. But you will. It starts on the upper floor first, and works its way down, through the walls."

"Towels are in the closet. I've got lots of towels. I took them from Dorothy when we split up. She loved to pile them in the bathroom, row after row of them, more than any two human beings could ever possibly use. Must have been deprived of towels as a child or something. So I took them. Petty cruelty."

"Don't sound so pleased with yourself—you mean man." Frank's voice hit a falsetto with the last three words. Though he meant it as a joke, for a moment Dorothy's face took up residence on Frank's face. I shook my head, and Frank returned.

"So tell me, buddy," Frank said, "how are you doing after . . . Jake and all."

I thought: If I could only tell you what else has been going on, you'd know the thing with Jake has shrunk to insignificance.

"It's a little bit lonely sometimes. I go to the door at night to take him out, and he's not there. You know, the usual sentimental crap." All true, but I had to fish for it.

"I know Brian misses him. He talks about him all the time. You know boys and dogs, especially neighbor dogs," Frank said.

"Too true," I said. "When I was a kid there was a dog that lived down the lane, near our summer cabin. I would stand on the back porch for hours the first day we arrived, waiting for him to come. Eventually he'd hobble over, and I'd feed him. He would come over every day after that, around sunset. Then one year, he didn't come; he had died the previous winter. I had a terrible vacation that summer; nothing seemed good that year—or after."

"Sad. I suppose you got over it," Frank said. I was not sure that I had; grief stuck to me. "Brian will have to get over it too. But he fights any sort of change. He's stubborn, like his mom. He would rather wallow." He paused, looked at his large hands. "I think he wants me to be the dog now."

Not such a bad call, I thought; Frank had a doglike affability, an animal solidity and faithfulness. I had felt it on our first meeting.

I let my inner smile show, faintly.

"What are you smiling at?" Frank asked perplexedly.

"Oh, nothing, just thinking about Brian and Jake—and everything."

He stood there with orange towels piled to his chin. "Nothing funny about it," he said irritably. "You try living with Brian."

"Sorry, it's my imbecile smile. I do that when I'm tired. I'm tired."

Frank walked to the door.

"I think I am beginning to understand what it's like to live with Brian," I said, half under my breath.

But Frank was already halfway up the stairs and didn't hear.

I was awakened in the middle of the night by a cry like a wounded child's: harsh, high-pitched, insistent as an auto burglar alarm. It kept on and on, until I had to put my hands over my ears.

The sound rose above the waves of wind and rain. Someone else will turn it off, shut it up, kill it: I'll be damned if I'm going out in the rain.

I went to the window. A dark shadow moved among the tangling shadows of tree branches on the balcony floor. So it wasn't a car or a psychotic kid in the alley. The shadow, at first a hollow outline, suddenly filled, became solid.

It was a half-drowned cat, squalling like a lost child.

I brought it inside.

I warmed up some milk. The cat eyed me from the kitchen chair, in its eyes a mixture of trust and suspicion.

I coaxed it out from under the chair by putting milk on my finger and leaving a trail to the bowl. The cat followed the trail, licking up the white droplets.

I got some towels from the hall closet. If the cat was tame, I would towel it dry. It was greedily lapping up the milk when I came back into the kitchen.

Waiting until it was done, I filled the saucer again. The cat watched from a discreet distance, then brushed affectionately against my hand, swatting it as I began to take it away.

"Okay, kitty, have it your way," I said, leaving my hand beside the bowl while it fed.

Later, I turned on the heater, laid the towel in front of it. The cat got comfortable. I was not going to be able to towel it dry without losing some skin in the process.

I still had kitty litter and a cat collar out back, which I had not had the heart to throw out.

I opened the back door, which looked out onto a shared porch and a dark window well; the rain beat out a steady rhythm on the gleaming garbage cans.

Above, a door opened, and Paul's unmistakable footsteps moved on the landing. I quickly grabbed the litter from the storage compartment and rushed back inside.

I filled an old dishpan with litter and put it in the bathroom. The cat made for it, scratched around, came out with a satisfied look on its face.

A faint tapping began on my back door.

"Michael," Paul said softly, though I pretended I didn't hear, "let me in."

Feeling like a child, I dived under the bed.

"What does he want?" I whispered to the dust.

"What he wants," came the voice from the curtained mirror, "is you."

"**H**e's getting out of control," Janette said. She wore no makeup. In her pale blue bathrobe she looked both old and young, like two people occupying the same body.

I stared at her, thinking about my grandfather's attic, where he had kept the ancient mirror, passed down from his father (and so on).

"Michael, are you there?" she asked petulantly, then shook my shoulder.

Janette and I had met in the lobby, getting our morning papers. She was rumpled, with a cup of steaming coffee tilted at a dangerous angle (but never spilling a drop); I was slopping my coffee all over the place, my body still shaped like ragged sleep. Come on over, I had said, thinking she wouldn't. But here she was.

"Sorry, I drifted off."

"Drifted off? You ask me how things are going with Paul, then you drift off? Some things are important. Like your question. Like my answer. You're not taking anything, are you?"

"Taking nothing," I said. "I just come and go sometimes. I've been tired."

"You do look a little under the weather. And your hair! I know hair coloring is the thing right now, but I liked you better as a blond."

She sat next to me, placing her slender-tough hand on my knee. "But to get back to Paul—that is, unless you've lost interest in your alter ego."

Alter ego? I bristled. Paul Marks and I had nothing in common; we could not be more different if we were man and wife. "Sure. Of course. You know I've been studying him. An enigma. Any information you could provide would be helpful."

Janette looked perturbed, tousled my hair, then drew back suddenly.

Was my hair dirty? Did it smell? Had she read my mind through her fingertips?

Then the apparition of Paul Marks, like hovering darkness, descended.

"Paul," Janette said, forgetting me, "is not an easy one to pin down. When I think I've got him figured out, he turns the tables on me. He's really good, really smooth. The transitions are so natural that he always seems to catch me off-guard. I pride myself on being an expert at, well, social matters. I've never met my match—until Paul. And that remains to be seen." She raised her hand to her chin thoughtfully, then her eyes lit up. "I've got it! A piece of the puzzle falls in place. Why haven't I thought of it before? He's found my weak spot, and reflects it back on me. Like a child who works his parents, causing them trouble when she knows more about them than they do. Like the child I was."

She paused, looked at me in a way that silenced my response. "It almost makes you believe in karma," she said. "Oh, God, if there is justice in the universe, then I'm finished." She laughed.

"Janette, I've never noticed that you have any weak spots," I said.

"You're just not interested enough to look for them." She seemed young again, a milky-skinned English beauty running out of a dark barn.

There had been a brief break in the rain. Light fell

through the prism of rain clouds. Janette's blue eyes were as intense and fathomless as the deep sea.

"Well, in that case, what is this weak link in your chain?"

She shifted uncomfortably, took her hand from my knee, then smiled. "If you think I'm going to let two people in this building know my secret, then you're crazy."

"Then, as far as I'm concerned, this conversation is merely theoretical."

A shadow leapt between us, grazing Janette's head and causing her hair to fall from the ribbon in which it had been loosely tied. It happened so quickly that it took me a second to figure it out.

"What the fuck was that?" she said, standing up and brushing her robe as though it had been soiled.

I looked behind the couch, pointed. "That's my new cat. No Name. That's his name. Found him on the porch the other night, half-drowned."

Janette glowered, fastened the belt of her robe more tightly, then straightened her neck. She was an old lady again.

"Where is the little beast?" she said, sitting back down, but at a distance. "Attacked me, the bloody bugger."

Then she started making clucking noises to entice the cat out of hiding.

"Won't work," I said blandly. "He only comes when he wants to."

"Don't underestimate my powers of seduction," Janette said, smiling from the left side of her mouth.

That cat didn't come out. But Janette kept up the clucking and cooing for several minutes.

"Come on, Janette," I said, getting bored. I wanted to be alone. "Give it up. When he thinks you don't care, then he'll come."

"Sounds like Paul Marks," she said acidly. "I wonder if he hasn't reprogrammed the whole building. Psychic plastic surgery."

I winced. "We've all got a little of that cat-and-mouse thing in us," I said.

She relaxed and stopped the seductive sounds. "I wonder how long this rainy spell is going to last. I have mixed feelings about it. One minute I feel divinely melancholy, the next trapped like a rat."

The cat made its entrance then, slinking about the walls, eyeing is suspiciously.

"There you are," Janette said, and then (one of the Paul Marksian smooth transitions, I guessed), "but really—who fucking cares?" She turned to me, poker-faced.

The cat approached under the coffee table and rubbed Janette's ankles. It was purring. It never purred for me. Janette pushed it gently but firmly away with a shapely foot. She crossed her legs and her fuzzy blue slipper hung casually from a bright red toenail.

Janette began bobbing the slipper above the cat's head, while she looked out the window. Wind blew water from leaves, which splattered the window.

The cat leapt crazily, trying to catch the slipper, but Janette kept moving it just out of reach.

I grabbed her foot, suddenly irritated. "Okay," I said, "you've tortured No Name quite enough. After all, he's an orphan." I knocked the slipper off her toe. The cat grabbed it gleefully, rolled over on it once, then walked away.

"You can't win," I said. "So you satisfy yourself."

The doorbell rang a little while later.

It was Patricia.

"You look awful," I said. "Come in." I took her arm. I could feel her pulse and sweat through the green angora sweater.

She watched me mutely, her mouth slightly open, lower lip trembling.

"I should be down there now," she mumbled. "But maybe it was my imagination. Whatever it is, I can't face it alone." She fell shivering into his arms.

"Patricia," I asked, "what's wrong?"

She pulled herself loose and went to the window, almost knocking Janette over.

"Well, hi to you too," Janette said sarcastically, but some instinct made her move out of the way.

Patricia pointed through the leaves and windblown rain, into the backyard. "Down there, something floating in the pool. I saw it from the landing window. Facedown. I think it's a body."

They said they'd be in touch.

"I wonder what they expect from us," Janette said suddenly, as she watched the detectives leave. "We found the body. We didn't put it there."

"They're just doing their job," I said. "There's no reason to suspect foul play. Brian was always playing around the pool. Frank said he had taught Brian how to swim when he was little, but I don't think he swam much because he always gave the pool a wide berth. Fear and fascination of water. He probably slipped and fell in headfirst and panicked." It was the most I had said since we found Brian. I felt odd suddenly, as though I were defending myself.

"Maybe he hit his head on something," Patricia said.

"Or maybe someone pushed him in," Janette said mysteriously. "Too much weird stuff in this building, all of a sudden. One of those clumps of pure awfulness." She looked up and down the walls, at us, then up the stairwell. For one crazy moment it seemed we became one blurry untrustworthy person. Janette's nose twitched; she scowled. "It's like it's coming out of the walls. Don't breathe or you'll drown," she said, and then disappeared up the stairs.

"Now, what do you suppose she meant by that?" Patricia asked.

"You should know," I said, not breathing. "It sounds like something you'd say."

* * *

Frank sat completely still for fifteen minutes; then a slow moan began, like wind in a hearth, and increased until he was crying. Then the grief began to heave, he swallowed it, was still for a moment, then the slow wave began again.

In a few minutes he grew still. I got him a cup of tea and closed the blinds. I sat next to him and gave him the card the detectives had given me.

He dutifully picked up the phone and dialed. His movements were stiff, robotic. They put him on hold for fifteen minutes; he stared at the receiver as though it were a snake that might bite him.

He nodded numbly into the receiver and hung up. "The detectives are out on another call," he said. "I'm to come down to the station to identify the body and sign some forms."

He looked at me helplessly. "Michael, will you go with me? I don't think I can drive."

"Sure, no problem," I said. He leaned forward and his tears sprayed my hand.

I thought of all the tiny reflections of my face, there in those droplets, if I only had eyes keen enough to see.

Patricia was sitting in the hall by Frank's open front door.

"Go downstairs and try to rest," I said. Frank stood behind me. Patricia's face was wrinkled and soft from grief.

"Go on," I insisted, putting my hand in the small of her back and pushing. "Try not to think about it. I'll take care of this."

I couldn't handle two basket cases.

Glancing at myself in Frank's hall mirror as I bundled him into his raincoat, I looked younger, darker, more alive than I had in years. Maybe it was simply that I liked being in charge.

Frank fumbled for his keys, dropped them, then fanned

through them as though searching for the one that would lock out the pain.

I heard a low moan, like night wind; then bass laughter and the careful closing of a door.

23

Frank had been right about the leaks eventually reaching me.

In the next few days the storms raced from the north, like troops marching. The gutters barely had time to drain the overflow that had turned the streets into rivers, before the next front arrived.

The walls creaked, strange smells were forced out by the moisture. Eventually a drip drip drip began near the head of my bed, a leak inside the wall.

I slept on the couch the next night, but a leak began there as well, next to my sleeping head inside the window frame, even louder than the other one.

Water followed me like a jealous lover.

I spent the following night back in bed with pillows jammed over my ears, trying to still my furious heart.

All night long, I thought of the zoo, Brian's fascination with caged animals, Frank's hatred of captivity. The images went round in an endless tape loop.

The rain continued to pour. The world got smaller and smaller. As it shrank, I pulled inward to avoid its touch. Soon I would be a tiny hard seed.

Days passed, night intervened, everything was dark gray. I followed my routines, never varying. I could not remember a time that was not like this. It went on and on, stretching like a blanket in all directions. I was like a child turned around in the dark, waking up and knowing nothing; finding only suffocation and fear.

Was there to be a future? Or had this featureless now consumed all possibilities?

On my days off, as I sat by the window, the pool seemed remote, unreal, a shape in a drawing, nothing capable of taking the life of a young boy. In fact, in this fuzzy indistinct world, it was hard to imagine anything happening; certainly nothing as acute as death.

I pictured the boy floating in the leaf-covered water. I pictured Frank, staring at the boy in the morgue, his face frozen, too afraid to feel. I pictured myself helplessly standing by, embarrassed and unsure what to say, what to do.

One night before I fell asleep, I jerked awake. I remembered what it was like to be married. I realized I was now alone.

I vaguely yearned to wake up next to someone. But first, I told myself, first you have to go to sleep.

Instead, I got up. I walked to the mirror, heavily, almost stomping. The pictures shook in their frames; No Name darted out from under the covers and hid behind the couch. Where were my apartment manners?

The walls shook.

I surveyed my tastefully apportioned room; my chest swelled. I ran my hands down my smooth belly, and walked forcefully to the mirror, head erect, back straight, as though I were coming down a runway in front of a panel of judges.

The mirror was covered by a curtain, a blue-and-white afghan my mother had sent me two Christmases ago. I pulled it aside, shutting my eyes, so that when I met my reflection it would be a surprise, like bumping into a stranger.

"Oh, hello there, so it's you. Haven't seen you in a while."

At first his image was not clear. I was angry, pounded the chilly glass, making my empty room shiver.

Then he slowly came into focus, smirking, fine-tuning himself, gaining edges and angles.

Vibrant, healthy, taller by the day. Broader shoulders too, fuller lips, dark red that was almost purple, a tick in his left cheek (masculine inner reserve), looking me up and down, while my eyes moved in the opposite direction.

I looked at him long and hard, trying to figure out what he was feeling. But I hadn't a clue. His face was like a dry mask grown into the bone.

"Did you have anything to do with Brian's death?" I asked, not expecting an answer.

A gust of wind hit the windows; the building shook like a toy in the hand of a willful child.

He continued to stare at me, as though he could not hear my voice; as though he were insensible to me. Yet I knew his indifference was a lie. I was his fascination, as he was mine. He was studying me and waiting—waiting for the right moment.

His feigned indifference made communication seem more urgent, and I fought down the familiar fire, the need to talk when no one was listening.

But the gust of wind had shaken something loose.

Water splashed my bare ankles. I looked up. A line of water followed a crack in the ceiling; soon the dark line swelled, like an overflowing river.

Then there was water everywhere.

By morning all that uncontrolled water had driven me into a frenzy. I'd been up all night mopping, emptying buckets, trying to do the impossible: feel dry in an inner-storming room.

I glanced furtively at myself while I was shaving; dark-eyed, shorter by inches. The effort had worn me down; had worn him down.

Or maybe the bigger, new me was hiding somewhere else, waiting. The thought made me shiver.

I cut myself while shaving; a very old disposable razor, with a broken stem. My face was haggard, old-looking. I pulled at my skin—loose and wrinkled, like a suit one has slept in. Around my mouth the laugh lines had become deep furrows, but they did not indicate laughter now; as though compensating for my constant nervous smile, the lines curved downward in what promised to become a permanent scowl.

I had just pasted some toilet paper to my bleeding face when the doorbell rang. I pulled on boxer shorts and went to the door.

"Have I got the wrong apartment?" Patricia asked, then shook her head, attempting a laugh. "The new Dark Michael. You look pretty muscular—but tired. Oh, well, I guess I've never seen you in the midst of a storm, in your underwear."

I nodded, knowing I was far from my best; my head felt like a crate packed with straw, the treasure having been removed.

"Could be," I said. "I usually wear loose-fitting clothes. Modest, you know."

"Mind if I help myself to some coffee? You look like you could use some too." She went into the kitchen. I listened to her footsteps, waiting for them to hit water.

"Ugh," she moaned, "you've got leaks too. Your kitchen floor is a mess. My feet are all wet."

I went to the kitchen. A leak from behind the stove had snaked its way across the linoleum: a mini-river. Patricia was mopping it up with a kitchen towel.

"I'm lucky," she said. "Only my back porch leaks. I have buckets out there. They fill up in a day." She stared up at me. "Hey, don't look so grim. It's only water."

"Only water," I said, "as in the drowning pool."

She paused and looked at her hands. "Poor Brian. I'll never forget that water coming from his mouth. Dead people look so small, don't they? And the way the head hangs, so limp and heavy—it's too awful to think about." She squeezed out the towel in the sink. "But this is different water, the rain we've been needing all winter, even though it's not really winter. We have to keep these things straight."

She mopped the floor very carefully, going over it several times, and plugged the apparent source of the leak. The coffee had begun to boil; there was a faint burnt smell.

With Patricia, you didn't have to say what you were thinking. She knew it before you did. It would be easy to get lazy in a relationship with Patricia. After a while, she'd be doing everything.

"Never boil coffee. Don't know why, but that's what they say." She poured two cups anyway. "At least it still has caffeine."

I drank, winced at the bitter taste.

"I talked to Frank," she said. "He's seen the police several times. They're haunting him, really." She got up, circled the kitchen twice, then stopped in front of the sink, looking down into the window well.

"Sit down," I said. "You're making me nervous."

"I'm sorry. I'm upset. I just heard something awful. Awful." She took two careful sips of her coffee. "Damn. Burned my tongue."

I waited.

"The news," I said impatiently. "Tell me what you heard."

"The police were talking to Frank when I came downstairs. I stood at the bottom and listened. They told Frank there has been evidence of foul play—apparently the autopsy showed that Brian had been sexually abused shortly before his death."

"Then he was killed."

"No, it doesn't mean that. It means that someone had been sexually abusing Brian. There was no trace of violence on his body, and the police quoted the coroner as saying that Brian—oh, how to put this and not sound horrible— had grown used to the sexual abuse. No torn tissue, nothing, He was ... well, stretched out."

"They don't think it was Frank, do they?"

"I didn't stick around long enough to hear, they were about to come up and I didn't want them to know I'd heard. But I don't think they would accuse Frank with no evidence. These things are very tricky. I know a couple in

Seattle who got divorced, the man freaked out, feeling rejected and impotent, and he and his new girlfriend molested his one-year-old daughter. The courts knew it, the psychologists knew it, but there was no hard evidence. The woman was a preschool teacher, and still is." Patricia's face clouded over. "Not that I think Frank would be capable of anything like that. Although I had known the guy up in Seattle for years, and never had a clue that he would be capable of such a thing. Which I guess goes to show that you can never know anybody completely."

I was only half-listening to Patricia, although I had laid a hand on her knee to convince her that she had my full attention.

I was thinking about the mirror my grandfather had in the attic of his big country house; it was where my father and his father kept their guns. My father had seen something in the mirror once, when he was a child, and was always terrified of going up there alone after that. I suspected what he saw was himself.

He always made me go get the guns for the dreaded hunting trips.

"Oh, not Frank," I said faintly. I would remove the cover from the mirror as soon as Patricia left, so that I could keep a closer watch on whatever it was that was adventuring under there.

"Oh, boy," I said, feeling cold, and a little afraid. "These last couple weeks have been the worst. One of those waves of pure awfulness that crest and then break. Maybe we're at the end of this one." I wasn't fooling myself; was I fooling her?

Patricia was silent; her head moved from side to side, her nose twitched. "No," she said finally, "I don't think so. There's something wrong. I think Janette may have had something when she said you could feel it coming out of the walls."

I nodded despondently, suddenly wishing she would leave.

I could hear rustling from the other room, and the curtain over the mirror wavering, as though a wind blew out from that silver world, a world that should always be still.

As she left, Patricia looked at me strangely, clinically. "We'll just have to wait and see what develops." She senses something, I thought; she would have made a good Jungian analyst.

When she was gone, I ran in to the mirror-wind. But it told me nothing.

It was Saturday. I went back to bed after putting towels under all the leaks. There was a distant pelting sound as water fell. I tossed and turned, now and then glimpsing my reflection, who was pretending to be me.

Eventually I fell into an uneasy sleep.

I dreamt water. I came home from school. No one was home. I got into the closet and put on one of mother's dresses. I shouldn't have, because I was overweight and I could feel the sickening tearing of the seams. But I was determined. Eventually I got into the dress.

I went to my room, barefoot. The furniture had been taken out, the posters torn down from the walls. There was a cloth blind over the window, pulled almost shut. A line of light illuminated a small black knob in the middle of the floor.

I closed the door, thinking that I heard my parents return.

Suddenly afraid, I tried to open the door. It was stuck. I grabbed the black knob in the middle of the floor and turned it. Something opened and water poured out. The room began to fill.

Underneath, the water moved; on its surface it seemed still.

When I could no longer touch bottom, I treaded water.

I rose with the water. The ceiling came closer. Mother's dress billowed about me. I tried to slip out of it but could not. I gasped for breath, and my face grazed the ceiling as I breathed the last of the air.

Finally the room filled completely, and I was under. My head bumped the submerged ceiling. The line of light from underneath the blind was the only light.

I could hold out only a moment longer. My lungs burned like fire. I dived to the center of the room and swam along the beam of light.

24

Frank awakened me from the dream of drowning. I always dreamt in the morning light, just before I woke.

"I don't mean to bother you," he said softly, standing in the doorway, shamefaced. "I sort of expected you not to be home. I thought I saw you go out last night, and I didn't hear you return."

No, I thought, he returns silently, invisibly.

"I've been sleeping here all night," I said, hoping it was true. Frank followed me to the living room. I pointed to my bed, which looked like a state of siege.

I quickly closed the door; in the lamplight, the knife beside the bed reflected red.

"Michael," he asked, "why the knife beside the bed?"

"Peeling oranges and stuff. Cutting cheese. I'm infamous for eating in bed," I said.

Frank looked puzzled. "Oh, I get it," he said understandingly. "You're nervous because Jake's dead. Not having a watchdog. I knew a girl once who used to sleep with a shotgun."

"No, it's not that—" I said nervously.

"Not that you're like a girl, I didn't mean that. Oh, I don't know what I mean. I just came back from visiting a court psychologist. I think he thinks I had been ... you know ... doing unnatural things with Brian."

Frank's expression moved from anguish to relief, then

back again. I suspected that somewhere between the conflicting feelings dwelt an untouched grief.

"You can't be serious," I said. "You? You're the most decent, upright man I've ever known. I'm sure this investigation is just a formality. I half-expect them to call me down for further questioning. They'll probably put us all through hell before this is over."

"Yeah, I suppose. But someone did molest Brian. That's a fact. Could have been one of his teachers, the father of a friend, an older friend I hadn't met . . . or . . ." Frank looked at the ceiling.

I tried not to notice. I remembered all too clearly the last encounter I had had with my upstairs neighbor. Inhuman power, seductive and pure, like a blade. Had he covered milk cartons with faces of children?

Perhaps he was to blame.

"I've never trusted that guy. And you said Brian had been spending a lot of time up there, sneaking out at night and stuff. A mentor, you said. Remember? I wanted to know what you thought—before I approached him. I know you've got a good ear for his moves."

"Have the police questioned him?" I asked.

"Just a little. Nothing much. Like they did for the rest of the neighbors. They don't seem to connect the molesting part with the drowning. That seems wrong to me, though I guess they know their job. Maybe Brian said he was going to tell, and the guy killed him, forced him under. I know it sounds crazy, but I think that's what happened. Brian was going to reveal the truth about someone, and that's why he's dead."

"What did Paul Marks tell the police?" I asked.

"That he knew nothing."

"Which may not be far from the truth."

"You'd think a father would cry when his son dies," Frank said, after building up to it for an hour or so. "I'm beginning to think that I did kill him." He wrung his hands in anguish. "What else could explain this"—he touched his chest—"this cold feeling? It's like a lump, indigestion, not sadness. Peg's back from Europe. She calls me every day, in tears. I try to put some feeling in my voice, but it doesn't sound real even to me. I know her. Unless I can share this pain with her, she's going to start blaming me. When I don't feel the way she thinks I should, that's how she gets. I hate to think what she'll do when she gets wind of the police investigation."

Frank looked at me hopelessly. He was trying to let out tear, but failing. The veins in his neck were distended. He looked like he would burst.

Hopelessly I put my arm over his shoulder. An electric charge passed through my arm. (It reminded me of the feeling when I had put my forehead against Jake's.)

The sensation rushed down my arm, into my neck, moved behind my eyes. I felt Frank's tear forming in my eyes; so I removed my arm.

"You know," Frank said through rasping breath, "I didn't love him. I have to admit it to someone. I didn't love him." He paused. "God, I said it. I remember one of the first nights after he had come home from the hospital. Peg was tired and I wanted to let her sleep. Brian had the colic, and was crying all the time. When I held him he cried even more. I wanted to throw him out the window."

"I never got along with my father either," I said. "It's unnatural, kids and fathers—like oil and water. What you're talking about isn't all that rare."

"In whose world? Not to love your own son, your own flesh and blood?" Frank scowled.

"Mothers have an easier time with children. There is something natural about that bond. Mother's milk and all of that. The relationship seems to work better. Children are like aliens to men. I'm sorry, but Brian got on my nerves. I hope that doesn't sound heartless, but what I mean is, I know how you feel. I'm glad Dorothy and I didn't have kids. Damn glad." My voice had started to rise.

"I hate myself for feeling this way—for not feeling anything," Frank said. "I hate myself."

"Well," I said, without thinking, "at least that's something."

I suggested we go jogging. Sometimes that pulled Frank out of his moods.

Frank tired out quickly and hurried home alone.

As I showered, I couldn't remember exactly who was grieving, and for what.

Grief seemed to be everywhere, like a poisonous cloud.

I sat down with the evening paper and tried to think; propped up my feet, which sometimes helped.

There was a splashing behind me but I didn't turn to see. I had run out of towels. Let the water go where it wanted. It's funny, I thought, but you can get used to anything. Like being dead; I wondered if you could get used to that. I barely heard the water now; yesterday it had seemed like a tidal wave.

I was through the paper in record time. Phantom news, flickering before my eye, making me feel vaguely connected with something. Was it the world?

One thought rose from my muddled mind: I had to face Paul Marks again. I had promised Frank to question him about his relationship with Brian. The problem was how to do it and still maintain my pride.

I stood up, letting the newspaper slide to the floor. The reflection in the rain-beaded window was that of a stranger. A tower of a man, equine facial structure.

I didn't have to remind myself who I was starting to resemble.

At twilight, through the shivering leaves, I saw a figure by the pool. I squinted, but through the foggy glass I couldn't tell who it was.

I went to my bedroom, stepped out onto the balcony, and looked down. The unidentified person dived in.

Filled with a sudden foreboding, I quickly pulled on pants and raincoat and rushed outside.

The rain was coming down in irregular waves. At the

edge of the pool I put up my hood, which the wind had blown from my head, and wiped my eyes.

There was a shivering movement, a man-size swell among the floating leaves and the splashing rain, at the opposite end of the pool. A shadow, underwater, swimming quickly toward me.

When the shadow got close, I reached under and grabbed hair. Frank's face came up, spitting water.

I helped him out, my hands under his solid arms. Grief had knocked him out cold. He was naked, blue as death, trembling. Black leaves clung to his flesh like leeches.

He squatted on the rim of the pool, holding his shin stubbornly against his chest and not looking at me.

I raised his face to mine, pulling against the muscles that held him in a knot.

When his eyes met mine, he began to cry.

We stood a long time together, swaying in the wind and rain, holding each other tightly, wondering where all the pain was coming from.

And if it would ever end.

Two weeks later, when the rains had stopped and spring was official, Frank's ex-wife came to visit.

Her voice shook the walls, and I tried not to listen; but I did listen, and so, I was certain, did everybody else in the building. We were all horrible gossips; and horribly concerned.

Why don't you hit me, she cried. To take it out on a poor innocent child. He trusted you. How could you? It's me you're angry with, not Brian. There was a deadly pause, then she began to cry in rhythmic sobs, like gunfire.

Frank's deep voice fell to a whisper. I could feel him disappearing, shrinking. It was as though a part of myself were being assaulted, and diminished. I wanted to rescue him, but knew that if I intervened, his anger would probably turn on me.

So I waited; and that tiny bit of me that was Frank grew faint and ill-shaped.

I paced back and forth. My place had gotten filthy; in the pale sunlit air dust rose, collided, fell.

Above my head, more pacing, a ghostly echo of my own, an unpleasant reminder that I would soon have to make a gesture of communication toward Paul Marks.

I walked through stale air to the front door. The foyer light had burned out. Visitors sometimes asked, "Were you sitting inside in the dark?" They couldn't see the light further in.

I heard Peg charge down the stairs. The emotions un-
furled like a cape, brushed my door. I could almost smell
the dishonesty, the tiny seed of real grief buried under all
that blame. Very dramatic, I thought; played to Frank, her
captive audience.

Glass rattled.

Frank plodded after her; his voice sounded like that of
a strangling child.

Damn you, I thought, applaud. She's a bad actress, and
if you weren't so trusting, you'd see it. Don't let her get
away with it.

You did nothing wrong.

Somehow I know.

The painting on my April calendar was a bluebird, winter blue, sitting on a bare branch.

I was sitting on the couch, drinking coffee, my only pleasure. The sky was pale, with high clouds, halfhearted
brushstrokes, signaling the start of another long dry season.

I didn't know what prompted the thought, but I realized
in a vague aching way, between heartbeats, that something
was missing. I stared at the bottom of the empty cup (spi-
dery cracks, stains that wouldn't come out) until it came to
me.

Nothing to cradle, no unquestioning love. Hadn't been
for days (for a decade). Had I grown so accustomed to ab-
sences?

I looked around the apartment, on the balcony, in the
backyard. I made stupid noises that always made him come,
but he didn't come.

I called but there was only silence.

No Name was missing.

There was a familiar voice in the hall. I couldn't attach
a name to it. The voice was associated with a warm feeling.
I was irritated.

I recognized Janette and Paul immediately. But who was
the third party?

I padded down the hall, resisted the impulse to lift the blind (hoping my shadow on the shade didn't give me away). When the hall was silent and presumably empty, I opened the door. Maybe my nose would tell me. Perfume, cologne, soap, and a slightly rancid smell.

I followed the echoes of footsteps (now inside Paul's apartment) back inside, to the balcony. Probably looking at the view. I didn't have a view. Three voices, words losing meaning as they dropped.

A butterfly flew up from the yard, landed on the peeling railing. I swatted it, catlike. It writhed, but did not die. It was black and yellow, an unusual variety, with wings as long as my thumbs.

I finished the job with a newspaper and blew the dusty residue into the yard. Insects were made of yellow powder weakly tied together by an illusion of beauty.

After a while, the bed upstairs started up, piston-thumping on my ceiling. My pulse started to pound as well.

I stared at the ceiling, wishing for the X-ray eyes of Superman.

I was horny, lonely. Feeling sorry for Frank had made it worse. I hadn't climbed the balcony since well before my sexual encounter with Paul Marks, but now I could not resist the narcoticlike pull.

What if he saw me, what if he asked me to join, what if I fell, what if . . . ?

Satisfaction, excitement, food for hungry eyes, was only a small climb away. Could I resist the temptation?

I put on a T-shirt, stood on the balcony awhile to see if I could be seen from across the way. No one visible; but there might have been telescopes in darkened rooms. I pulled myself slowly outside the balcony, reached the familiar first handhold, then the next.

Before I knew it, I was there. I paused below the level of sight, listening. They would not notice me; they must be blind as bats, in the middle of that most moving of trances.

I pulled my eyes up to, then over the edge.

"Well, hello there," Margaret said, sitting in a white wicker chair and reading a newspaper.

"Is my cat up here?" I said. I almost lost my grip. "I'm looking for my cat."

"Hmm," she said. "Why don't I come down and we'll talk. While they finish up. And be careful you don't fall."

"Don't be embarrassed," Margaret said as I ushered her in. "Gonadal thinking is what I call it. Most men can't control themselves at times. It must be terrible."

I was still denying my attempted voyeurism, but Margaret wasn't buying. She didn't press the point, however.

"I haven't seen you around since the barbecue. What a disaster that turned out to be."

"Oh?" she said, mildly surprised. "I had a rather good time."

"Maybe you left before it all happened. My dog mistook me for a burglar and went for my throat. I ended up spending the night in an emergency room with a transvestite who had taken an overdose of pills and a smelly old woman who said she had dead kittens in her bag. I guess she was there for psychiatric help."

"Oh, no! Really? Janette didn't say a thing about your problem. The last thing I heard about you was Paul Marks saying something about there being two of you, one down, one up. Then I left. I was tired. I get tired a lot lately. I think it's in the air. Effect of atomic testing or something." She paused.

Margaret smiled a dazzling smile, as if trying it out, then closed her mouth, suddenly self-conscious.

"Do you think I'm beautiful?" she asked, out of the blue.

"Of course," I said. "That's more than obvious."

"The other day I went into a store and smiled at the man behind the counter. I wanted a pack of cigarettes. He gave me the cigarettes, then asked me why I smiled all the time. I didn't know if he thought I was flirting with him. He was a strange little man, short, with crazy bright eyes. You know the type— they're all over the place since they've cut back on the in-patient beds in the mental hospitals. Anyway, I haven't been able to smile without thinking of what that man said. I'm confused. That's why I asked. I hate being beautiful."

She was staring across the room, into an unlit corner. "Do you have something to drink?"

I nodded.

"There's nothing beautiful about being drunk; it's universal. Is that the refrigerator?"

"Pardon the mess. It's dark back there, so I don't keep it too clean."

She went to the refrigerator, disappeared behind the open door, came out with two beers, one dark, one light.

"How symbolic," she said.

She had hair like still water under moonlight. A cloud of lilac enveloped her, leaving delicate traces as she moved. Not overpowering, but pervasive. When she sat down, I resisted an impulse to put my arm around her; she seemed to require it, like a plant that needed rain. For that reason alone, I did not.

"About your cat," Margaret began. "I don't know what exactly is going on, but ..."

"Oh ..." I said, getting the bottle opener.

"Paul Marks has a new cat, and I think it's your cat. He seems to know it's yours too, and is playing a little game. I think he wants you to come up and ask him for it."

She took a long thoughtful swallow of beer; moisture lingered on the sharp curve of her upper lip.

My heart sank at the news about No Name. After a while, and half a bottle, I said, "Oh, really. I'll have to go up and talk to him about it."

"As far as I know," Margaret said, "he hasn't done any experiments on it yet, like putting a dog's head on it or anything. You know those surgeons have to alter everything according to some secret inner plan."

"Some good news at last. But what were you doing up there anyway, while Janette and Paul were ...?" I asked.

"Not watching. That's what I do. I'm the third party, who's supposed to give their sex life a lift. I don't mind.

I've accepted that they're both crazy, so I read the newspaper."

"Don't you feel taken advantage of?" I said, reminded of an incident with a married couple before I had met Dorothy; they had used me to rekindle their thinning sex life, then dumped me.

"Advantage? No, I'm not involved in it. It's their problem." She smiled broadly; I resisted looking at myself in her teeth. "And another thing," she said, finishing her beer and shaking the bottle, "I bet Janette has told you some untruths about us. Like she and I are lovers. Like you are the only one to know both sides of her, besides me." Her smile had disappeared, replaced by a faint sneer.

"Yes, she did. Right after I met her and before—"

"And before you went to bed with her," Margaret finished. "Didn't you think that odd? That she was a lesbian, and immediately seduced you?"

"Bisexual?" I offered timidly. Margaret shook her head. "Just real friendly?" I had begun to smile, then to laugh.

"She figures if she tells a man something about herself that no one else knows, he will trust her immediately. Trust is what she is after—but she likes to steal it. The lesbian thing is a turn-on to most men."

"Oh, no . . . oh, no," I kept saying until Margaret put a damp hand over my mouth.

"Don't feel bad. *Many* have fallen for her line. Including me, in a different version."

"You?" So I didn't know Janette after all. The news was not as distressing as it might have been. We all had secrets. "How so?"

"Well, when we first met, Janette told me she had been an abused child. A stepfather or something. I felt complete sympathy; there is nothing, believe me, *nothing*, that brings women together faster than stories about abuse. I had had a similar experience, though not as bad as the one Janette described. The girl has a great imagination. She said she didn't like men, that she wished she could be open sexually with a woman, but hadn't been able to up to now. I had worked off some energy with a couple of girlfriends in college, but really didn't consider myself even vaguely bisexual. Before I knew what was happening, she was seducing me. Not sexually; I never did feel any of that for her. Well, at least not much. But I did lose interest in my then-current boyfriend. And my relationship with Janette became so intense that I couldn't think of anything else." She paused, her eyes gone cold. "Maybe that's why you thought we were together. We are close, tied up. But I think I have the heavy end of the chain."

The thumping upstairs had ceased. There was running water, scampering bare feet.

"Of course there was no stepfather. And Janette loves men. She wishes she were one," Margaret said.

"So why do you put up with it?" I asked. "What do you get out of it?"

"Don't know. For want of better. My relationship with my boyfriend really was fucked. Janette mirrored that back to me. She is bright, you know. And if you look at her long enough, you learn something—if you have the strength."

"What is Paul learning?" I asked.

"Paul doesn't learn. I don't think he sees anything when he looks into her mirror."

The doorbell rang and rang. Margaret and I had gotten drunk. We stared at each other, smiled like two children hiding under the bed, and did not answer.

Let Janette wonder for once.

Finally the ringing stopped, the front door slammed, and a car roared off.

"Revenge," Margaret said, "is bittersweet. I feel that I'd better go after her and apologize. She knew I was down here. The woman has supernatural hearing."

I was disappointed. "You have nothing to apologize for. Imagine making you watch her have sex with Paul, as a turn-on. If she can't get Paul into bed without your help, I'd say her power over him is finished."

"Well, I didn't mind. I was in a weird mood but I agreed.

Janette can be convincing, even when I know she's using me. Sometimes it's easier just to give in." Margaret stood up woozily.

"My," she said, "we have been sitting for a long time, haven't we?"

I felt as if I had become part of the furniture. Margaret offered me a hand up.

"Margaret, I'm glad we got to talk. I like Janette, you know, really I do—despite herself, if you know what I mean. But I like you more. You're the same, only not really. I hope I'm not offending you."

"You aren't the first to mention it," Margaret said, picking up her coat and walking carefully to the door. "Janette and I are twins. She is the evil one, which makes me the good one, I guess."

"Nice running into you," I said, and she left.

26

Frank had not gone to work for a week. Patricia had done her best to lure him out, but with little success. I had gone up a couple of times, though it hurt me to see Frank in so much pain. I doubled over with it, clenching my stomach, while trying to tell him to cheer up.

I'm afraid I didn't paint a very convincing picture.

The building had been quiet as a tomb the past week. Paul Marks was either gone or gestating (I suspected the latter). Flowers had begun to bloom in the yard, on the street, unlikely waxy blossoms that looked like props for a science-fiction movie. The tree branches were loaded with the pendulous things, red spheres that became needles up close, with tiny yellow flowers whose pollens erupted into the air.

The air smelled like a cheap whore; my nose stuffed up, my mouth grew dry and cracked. I felt like a walking desert.

I wanted to close the windows but I had to keep the balcony window open in case No Name tried to climb back down.

I took antihistamines, but couldn't stand the mental fog. The real fog would be back soon enough. So I stopped taking anything and decided to live with not having a usable nose.

In a few days there would be a street fair. Patricia had been working on Frank about going. An outing, just for the three of us. Who had endured the hells of a hellish winter, and survived.

Frank at first said no, then said maybe, then yes, when I asked him nicely and told him I wouldn't go unless he did too.

The day arrived. Pale blue sky, no clouds, faintly oily breeze, the smell of baking dogshit under palm trees.

There were cars parked all over the sidewalks, kids driving slowly by in open-topped Cadillacs, a general surge up the hill, into the blue and beyond.

I waited on the front stoop for Patricia to come down. She was invariably late, but Frank was always later. I wondered if she was having trouble getting him out of his place.

Maybe in the open air, with the roar of people and distractions, some of Frank's grief would dissipate. We had been living inside too much, and needed an airing, like stale furniture or curtains soiled with months of closed winter air.

Patricia pulled Frank down the stairs. He looked downcast, but brightened a little when our eyes met. Patricia wore a white sweater and baggy gray shorts; Frank was bundled up for winter: sweatshirt, sweater, heavy pants, and hiking boots.

"Frank," I said, grabbing his arm. "You're going to boil in those clothes."

"Oh, all right," he said, like a pouty child, and started to disrobe. He peeled down to a bright pair of boxer shorts and a black T-shirt while we stared.

"Very fashionable," I said, "but the underwear is a little bold, don't you think?"

"You said it was warm."

"Not that warm. I have a pair of walking shorts I think will fit you." The idea of Frank wearing my clothes pleased me.

I ran upstairs and got him the shorts and a lightweight shirt. He slipped them on as though they were his own.

Patricia, standing outside with her hands on her hips, was watching passersby suspiciously. "If this is any indication of the crowd, we're in for a mighty fine time," she said facetiously.

"Oh, you can't estimate an ocean by a drop of water," I said. "Let's go."

"In which direction?"

"Follow the herd," I said.

I was reminded of the barbecue, my last social outing. When there is so little space, why do people huddle all the more? Isn't there anyone who is going to the street fair alone?

And, I thought, putting my arms around Patricia and Frank, do these people really like each other? Or are they just insurance against being alone?

I told myself not to think too much; and started to enjoy the walk, and the sun. My armor cracked a little bit, and the sun crept in.

But by the time I got to the top of the hill I was starting to feel sick.

"Oh, come on," Patricia said. "You'll make it. You're unused to the sun is all."

Ahead, there were several blocks that had been cordoned off; it was wall-to-wall people.

Frank looked great, his skin had taken on color, his walk was brisk and confident. We had exchanged moods, somehow. (I wondered if I should ask him for my clothes back.)

"We're going into that?" I whined. "Why, in God's name? We won't be able to move."

"It not as bad as it looks. Once you're inside, you just sort of flow with the crowd. Here, follow me. Mommy will show you how." Patricia took my shaking hand and Frank followed, chuckling.

Down the hill we went. My stomach was in my mouth. I looked back at Frank. He had taken off his shirt and was smiling broadly. I could see he was pleased no longer to be the object of pity.

"I don't know what's come over you all of a sudden," Patricia said. "One minute bright, the next moody as hell."

There were barbecues somewhere, though I couldn't see them. The smoke overhung everything, sourceless, cloying. I had almost forgotten it was a sunny day; nausea always turns me into a monster.

We couldn't easily get to the sides of the street where the concessions were. I saw the backs of people, colorful summer-clothed people, row after row of them, facing smoking caldrons.

"There must be a reason," I started to say, but Patricia pulled my arm sharply.

"If you don't cheer up, I'm going to spank," Patricia said. "Don't look, just feel. It's a nice day, all these people are having fun. Don't think about them as individuals. Give yourself a break. I don't want to sound Pollyannaish, but there is a time to give the old noodle a rest." She tapped my swimming forehead with a red-tipped finger.

"You've certainly changed your tune," I said, giving Patricia up as hopeless; maybe I could cajole Frank into sharing my misery. Guilt was welling up inside me, like bile rising in my throat. I would choke on it, I would drown. "Frank, have you heard from Peg anymore?"

Frank looked at me blankly, smiled. "No," he said. "And I don't care to."

Well, that was that.

Frank moved back slightly, making his refusal doubly apparent. As he withdrew, something was drawn out of me. I was light-headed yet I felt I might burst.

As I followed Patricia, I wondered if the woman who had looked like her, the powdery mask of a woman, was dead. And who had stilled Brian? Were there others, still buried in memory?

Parents would forgive; Patricia would forgive, though maybe Frank would not. What forgiveness could I expect from the face in the mirror?

"Michael, old friend," Frank said, thumping me hard on the back, "snap out of it. As soon as I put on your shorts, you started acting funny. I'll take them off if you like."

"Frank," Patricia said mock-sternly, "if you drop your

drawers—Michael's drawers"—she liked to be precise—"I'll scream."

I spotted a chemical toilet and made straight for it.

"I have to use the bathroom," I said urgently.

"You don't look at all yourself," she said, helping clear a path.

"Excuse me," she said to an obese woman who was waiting in line. "My friend isn't well."

The woman moved quickly out of the way when she saw my face.

The door opened, a young boy smiling contentedly came out. I brushed past him. He gave me a dirty look. I slammed the door, then leaned on it, protected from the outside by the weight of my body.

I was safe. I wondered if I could convince myself to go back outside. The dark was nice, and small.

There was an oval mirror over the chemical toilet. I looked at my face: squinting, glassy eyes, patterns of lines I did not recognize as my own. The signature of whose experience?

I leaned on the mirror. The surface was cool against my forehead, solid. The surface released, turned liquid, then to nothing. A man-shaped vacuum beckoned.

I fell through and occupied the space.

I was inside, he was outside. He looked well, his face free of lines, of any expression really, though he smiled. I felt like a depository for the unpleasantness he did not wish to contain; frozen behind glass, and miserable.

He winked at me, then opened the door to a blaze of light, and joined Patricia and Frank.

"Oh, you're looking much better," I heard Patricia say.

Someone new shouldered his way in; the door closed and I was blind.

I waited. A couple of people came in; it was too dark to see clearly, and anyway, I tried not to look. They used the facilities, then left.

Then, in the blinking of an eye, I was outside in the

light, seeing my counterpart staring at me, at himself. I looked out from the reflective surface where I had been transplanted, into his sunglasses, and saw that I was an image in a silver balloon. Apparently when he saw himself, I could see as well.

Mirrors, I thought, mirrors are linked in some underneath way, being part of a collective, an ocean of mirrors that is really only one.

Since I knew the intensity of my friend's self-involvement, I could anticipate spending a lot of time out of the john and in the thick of things.

The world seen from the balloon was distorted, smeary and melting. Like looking into a carnival mirror, only worse, because as the balloon bobbed in the wind, so did the world: I got seasick on the wind. Being lighter than air had its disadvantages. I imagined this was what it would look like when the bomb was dropped. People coming apart, merging into one another, colors blurring, shapes pouring their contents out until people and things were empty shells.

After a while I got used to it. The distortions distracted me from my powerlessness. Like a drug, something that would leave you in time. But interesting, at least for now. My counterpart followed the balloon around, mesmerized by his image.

Frank and Patricia were deep in conversation and hadn't noticed the change in me. It was amazing how friends sometimes could not see the screamingly obvious about you. My counterpart's self-absorption may have seemed a welcome return of strength.

Patricia and Frank approached, grabbed his arm.

"Michael," she said, "you seem taller. What happened in that bathroom? Some kind of instant ego builder?"

"Natural processes bring you back to yourself," my counterpart said slyly, "if you know what I mean. When I was a kid I stooped so people wouldn't notice me. This is my real height. Let's see if I can maintain it."

Was he planning to leave me trapped in the mirror world?

"I think it's time we moved on," Frank said. "I want to get away from those damned balloons. They remind me of Brian. Heart-shaped silver balloons. He'd bring them home and watch them deflate. And wouldn't throw them out even then."

"No mention of Brian today," Patricia said. She was keeping her voice bright and cheerful.

She pulled a pin from her bag and stuck it into the balloon where my face was.

I was back in darkness.

I waited. People passed through the john, united at least by that common self-expression. I tried thinking about other things while the creative act was occurring.

Two men came in together. This time I watched.

"Hurry up," one of them said. "People are waiting."

"Oh, yeah," the other one moaned as they hurriedly unzipped. The one guy lit a Bic lighter. Their erections flopped out, flickering shadows made huge by the flames.

"Here, I've got some rubbers," the smaller man said, reaching into his coat pocket. His eyes were fixed on the other man's hardening penis as though it revealed the meaning of life.

"Not with a rubber, buddy," the other one said. He opened the door, stormed out.

The small guy blinked into the light of the open door. He was standing in full view of the crowd, trying to hide his erection, an apologetic smile on his face.

My counterpart had struck up a conversation with a young woman. I peered out her sunglasses.

It was a dizzying experience: I had a face in each lens, and therefore two sets of eyes to see with.

There had been too many people anyway; now everyone had a twin.

"So," my counterpart said, "do you live in the city?"

"I was born here."

"Really? A native? Unusual."

"Someone has to be born here," she said rather petulantly.

"I suppose so," he said. "It's just that you seem so normal. More of a corn-fed girl."

"Oh, I see. Meaning that San Franciscans are in some way abnormal. Corn being the standard for normal."

"Now, don't get huffy. I mean that people here take eccentricity for granted. If you aren't eccentric, then they are suspicious of you."

He put a hand on her shoulder. Her eyes were more bored than angry. She didn't move away. There were two of everything, but I tried to forget that and fuse them in my mind. I was successful only to a limited extent.

"What I mean is, here everyone is so complicated. You don't seem complicated."

"We're all complicated in our ways," she said. She was looking him up and down, with a dull hunger.

He had spread his feet slightly, and was looming over her, like a predatory bird, like two predatory birds.

Frank and Frank and Patricia and Patricia entered the picture.

"Who's your new friend?" Patricia asked.

My counterpart looked irritated. "I don't know your name," he said to the girl.

She didn't get a chance to answer.

There was a sudden commotion, a sharp noise, the collective intake of breath. The girl looked away from my counterpart toward the source of the disturbance.

The last thing I saw, before I fell back into the darkness, was a flood of people, shoulder to shoulder, surging, and a baby stroller being knocked over as they ran from whatever it was they thought chased them.

I could think of a million things.

* * *

The darkness was as thick as tar. The chemical toilet smelled bad. Tissue paper littered the dark floor like wilting flowers, glowing faintly.

I waited. My counterpart would come back in. He had been drinking a lot of beer and I knew his bladder capacity only too well.

I called to him, sent out shivering messages from the mirror. People came and went, leaving their signatures in the atmosphere. They all merged into one bad smell.

I flickered outside briefly, once, twice, I guess from windows of parked cars. But he was moving, never stopping long enough for me to orient myself.

I waited for what seemed like an eternity. He might never come back. I had no way of knowing. I tried not to think about it.

Finally the door opened and a familiar stranger came in. My counterpart had returned and he had the blond girl with him.

He unbuttoned her blouse, began to fondle her breasts. He unzipped his pants and tried fucking her.

"Hey, give me a second," she said. "I'm as dry as a bone."

"Oh," he said in a voice as flat as glass. He turned her around in one sharp movement, and penetrated her rectally.

"Hey, haven't you heard of AIDS?" she said, trying to pull away. When it was clear that she couldn't struggle free, she said, "I'm not the one in ten who enjoys this."

He let out a single grunt, then came.

At that moment, I was face-to-face with the cold-eyed girl, who looked to be about eighteen. My counterpart had returned to the mirror.

"I'm sorry," I started to say, "I don't know what came over me."

"Where the hell have you been?" Frank demanded. "We've been looking all over for you. I was worried. This crowd is pretty weird. Lucky that little panic a while ago didn't crush the baby. Someone on drugs started to freak,

172

and people got panicked and started to push. Too many people, too little space."

"I was wandering about. Nowhere in particular. Lost in the crowd."

Patricia looked at me quizzically. "You've shrunk about three inches again. You have the most moody body of any man I've ever known."

We started to snake our way through the crowd, toward home. The sky was clear. A rusty color spread from the horizon as the sun dropped out of sight.

"Look, over there!" Patricia said, her voice full of scandal. "Unless I'm mistaken, that man in the center of the circle of adoring young ladies is Dr. Paul Marks. Looking for clients, no doubt."

Before I could stop her, she was dragging us in his direction. "Neighbors should be neighborly. Besides, one of the people he's talking to is the wife of a director at ACT. I auditioned for a part. Let's go mingle, and maybe I can do myself a little good."

"Patricia, you're two-faced," I said, pleased to be in good company.

"Perhaps," she said thoughtfully, still moving. "But I think I still know which one is real."

27

I had notched the wooden frame next to the mirror as I grew in height. Today I made a mark near the top; soon I'd be over the top, my head out of sight. Eventually I imagined I might grow, like a beanstalk, right through the ceiling.

My counterpart steadfastly held his hand to his side and glared at me while I notched the wood.

Did he feel trapped? As I had felt when I was lost in that temporary toilet? Revenge was sweet.

Paul Marks was upstairs with a new woman; I had watched them come in as I got my mail. He had hurried her upstairs, mumbling hello.

She was unattractive, overweight, with a doughy face. He had good reason to be embarrassed. She had seemed all too human. A candidate for surgery?

I dropped my clothes and masturbated for the mirror. As I was about to come, I pressed my finger under the shaft and stopped the flow. I did not want to soil the mirror.

I limped into the bathroom and let it go into a towel.

Then I watched an episode of *Barnaby Jones*, half-listening for Paul's signature moves. It was dead quiet.

What could be going on? The embarrassment of encountering Margaret on my last climb restrained me from scaling the building and taking a look.

The new woman had looked like a nurse. Was Paul Marks in need of care? The concept of him needing another human being was not only unlikely but also somehow repulsive. The idea soured in my mind.

Undoubtedly his attentions would trap her imagination for weeks, months to come, and fill those diary pages. She looked the type who would never love anyone who would love her back.

Eventually there was some faint stirring, definitely suggestive, though not the usual piston-engine pumping that meant everything was full steam ahead.

I thought about the street fair while listlessly wiping myself clean. When Patricia had dragged us into Paul's circle, he had barely looked at me. I had been sure our seminal encounter had been a prelude to something more ominous, more permanent, at least in his mind.

His lack of acknowledgment somehow had made me feel powerful, and I had stared at him relentlessly, until he began to squirm and excused himself shortly after.

I masturbated again. The movements of my hand were mechanical, mildly frantic, and when I was finished, my hand didn't want to stop.

Suddenly there was a crashing sound, like a body falling, shouted words that blurred as they reached me. I felt dry as sand. There was anger; it oozed through the floor.

What I guessed was a hasty putting-on of clothes; there was the sound of Paul's door roughly opened, heavy steps on the stairs; Paul running after, his voice pleading, begging.

"I'll be more gentle. I can change. I can learn." Who was this stranger masquerading as Paul?

Filled with contempt, I turned up my TV to drown out the noise.

"Janette," I said, "you and Paul are like this." I held two fingers together. "Who was the dumpy girl he had up there earlier, the pale one who looks like a nurse?"

"Michael, you're awfully callous today." Janette seemed old; it looked good on her. A motherly quality I found subtly attractive. "It was probably his sister. Paul doesn't know many women who aren't stunning. Present company not excepted."

"His sister?"

"She's the only person in his family he ever talks about with any feeling. Dad is a good man, Mother is a peach, but there's no feeling in his voice, like he's saying it because that's the image either he has made up for them or they've hammered into him. But baby sister—she's another story. I think maybe they slept together once."

My heart raced. "I think they did it again today, earlier. They had a big fight out in the hall afterward. I'm surprised you didn't hear it. Paul pleading. It was hysterical."

"Michael, I don't know what has gotten into you. I didn't hear the fight because I wasn't home. And if I had been home ... I try to give my neighbors a little privacy." She looked at me suspiciously. "You are the busiest little bee when it comes to other people's affairs, aren't you?" and she tweaked my cheek rather hard.

I fought back a brittle anger.

"You and Paul have been out for each other since the first day. Don't you think it's time you gave it a rest? Go up and fuck him. That's what I do, and he's no big threat." She was lying, of course; suddenly she seemed more a cartoon character than a woman.

I appeared to listen intently. I went to the bar and poured us drinks without asking. I knew lately Janette was trying not to drink, but I wanted to loosen her tongue.

I set the tumbler down in front of her. A beam of sunlight struck the glass. The amber glow seemed to reach out like a hand.

I took a calculated sip, a slow burn, turned to her with moisture still clinging to my lips, which were parted slightly, and blew faintly in her direction.

She looked at me irritably, crossed her legs, and sat back, staring at the ceiling.

"Oh, I forgot," I said convincingly. "You're not drinking anymore, are you?" Janette had shouted from the rooftops when she discovered that she was an alcoholic, an addictive personality. She wore her newfound sobriety like a badge.

As I gestured to remove the glass, the stopped me with a strong grip.

"One won't hurt. I hate to see you drinking alone." Her face bunched up like a closing hand.

Janette watched herself pick up the glass, distractedly, as though someone else were doing it.

"Go on, a little one won't hurt you." And I helped her lift the glass to her lips.

"Oh, God, what's that?" Janette rolled over in bed, an alcoholic fog pouring from her mouth; beneath that, a sour sleep smell. I turned away. "I must have fallen asleep."

"Passed out is more like it," I said, watching her bleary face intently for any sign of pain.

She sat up, sweat beading her upper lip, her breasts bobbing as she tried to catch her breath. She reached under her.

"Michael," she said, pulling the knife out from under her body, "how did this get into bed?" She threw the knife across the room; it sailed out the window and landed on the balcony.

"And furthermore, what am *I* doing in bed?" she asked, her voice rising in indignation. "My head hurts. I don't remember a thing."

I looked at her. "Oh, come on, you kept saying my name, begging me to do things. Don't play cute with me."

"Michael, you're really pissing me off." She leaned forward; her left breast grazed the comforter. "Ouch, what happened here?" She looked down at a nipple that resembled a wilted rose.

"I don't know," I said. "You were really crazy. I responded in kind. I wonder if you mistook me for Paul Marks in the frenzy of your amour."

"You get me drunk and into bed, with you and that fucking knife, and you dare to call me crazy." She was examining her breast in the bedside light, a ferocious look on her face.

"You practically tore it off," she said, her voice full of rage but verging on tears.

I waited for the tears.

They never came. She leapt out of bed, threw the covers over my face.

"I hope you find someone who uses that knife on you," she said, following the trail of her clothes back to the living room, putting them on piece by piece.

The door slammed; there was wind. I looked over at the mirror, where I had removed the curtain to watch the sex.

The man inside the mirror was crying.

I pulled the curtain over him.

"I know this might sound strange," Patricia said, sitting on the far side of the couch, "but I am starting to like Paul Marks."

I paused long enough for her to absorb my cold disapproval. She wasn't receiving today, which sometimes happened when her mind was set. "I'll pretend I didn't hear that."

"Pretend whatever you like, Michael. But it's the truth. And it's not just because he has connections with the theater company."

"I didn't say anything."

"You don't have to. I can see it in your eyes." (No, I thought, you cannot; that is not what is there.) Her face turned icy and her eyes blazed; she looked like she would get up. Then didn't. She smoothed her skirt, a habit that indicated she was having conflicting impulses. I used to find that motion endearing, childlike; today it seemed indecisive.

"Michael, I've wanted to talk to you ever since the street fair. You seem different toward me. Is there anything I've done that's made you angry? You look mad all the time. You even walk differently. When I'm on the street and I see someone walk like that, I go to the other side of the street." She waited, drumming her fingers on her knee.

I didn't say anything, but counted the seconds, each one silent, unfilled. Eventually they passed.

"I haven't got all day, Michael. If you don't want to talk now, we'll do it another time. I've got to go upstairs." She looked embarrassed, then indignant. "I promised Paul to bring him something. To return a record I borrowed."

"So you've fallen into his clutches too?" I said dramatically, and got up.

"Go or stay," I said in her general direction. "It doesn't matter to me."

And I went out for a walk, leaving the door open behind me.

The houses on the top of the hill seemed more solid than the ones below. From there, a clear view of Twin Peaks: a woman's breasts, a sleeping woman. A shimmering necklace of lights adorned her.

I wondered what it would be like if she would wake and stand and shake us off.

I remembered a time when the lights had been off all over town. The streetlights, everything. It was dusk, and driving through the unlit streets in rush-hour traffic as the primordial dark shrouded the city had been eerie, exciting. As I drove down Market Street toward the peaks, which had not known such darkness for fifty years, I thought if there were a time for the sleeping woman to stand and begin to walk, that was it.

But she did not. Was she dead?

Eventually the lights had come back on, and normal routine was restored.

For two weeks I could not shake the depression that had settled on me when the lights had come back on.

I walked to the end of the highest block, then back down the other side. The block was short, every house as pretty as a wedding cake; you never saw anyone on the sidewalks, and the windows were curtained, shuttered, usually dark.

I walked around the highest block twice, checked a For Rent sign that said no pets, although I knew I couldn't afford it.

The higher you went, the higher the price.

Anyway, I couldn't move into the place—maybe No Name would come back. At the street fair, I asked Paul if he had seen my cat. He said he hadn't, though he'd been taking care of a friend's cat while she was out of town.

"Here, kitty," I said, clucking and purring into the darkness when I got home. "Come here."

He wouldn't just come home on his own, I thought. Miracles don't happen. Paul has probably taken him to the pound, or thrown him into an alley, where a racing car has flattened him.

I searched the apartment thoroughly anyway.

Feeling a confusing mix of emotions, I started to search for an old shoe box.

Then I went down to the garden and buried the empty box.

Patricia was upstairs. It took me a while to figure it out. I knew her steps on the stairs, but they were out of place up there.

I lay in bed and let the anguish pour over me. If Patricia had given in to Paul Marks, then what hope was there for me?

Ripping the curtain from the mirror, I looked. Only a reflection, a trick of light on a flat silver surface, nothing more.

I challenged him to a pantomime; but of course, sensing my need (if he could sense; if he ever had, outside my imagination), he did not respond.

I moved, I moved, I moved: there was nothing else.

What were they doing upstairs? It was too quiet. I started up the side of the building, but came back down. Too humiliating; she would feel sorry for me if she saw, and she might be looking, because she knew me.

She walked softly—I had to listen hard to hear her—as though trying to disguise her footsteps. Was she being considerate of my feelings, or deceptive?

Where was Paul? In bed, waiting?

The ceiling creaked, first over here, then over there. I

imagined she was doing a dance for him, slowly dropping her clothes.

She really wants me, I thought. Part of me has swum upstream, upstairs. She doesn't realize it yet, but what she is drawn to is me, something I've lost.

I thought of how I had rebuffed Patricia that night, weeks ago. I could now be in Paul Marks's shoes if I had been more demonstrative of my feelings.

Or perhaps I had been.

I closed my eyes.

I spun, my head fell to the pillow, then through.

Something came over me. It dropped out of the air, heavy, slightly damp; I thought of sails collapsing in a storm.

Smothering, I tried to move my hands against the weight, but the canvas stuff was too heavy. It was dusty-smelling, yet damp with mold.

Was I asleep or awake? Or caught somewhere in between?

My first thought was that someone had crawled in the open window, a prowler, and was trying to murder me.

He had his hands over my mouth, and the heavy weight of his body pinned me down. I could not see, because he had pushed my face into the pillow.

His heavy hot breath panted against my neck, his saliva like a net dropping over my hair.

I struggled, but he was powerful. As he held me, he pulled back the covers, exposing my naked body to the damp night wind.

His hands closed around my throat. I tried to scream, but could not; choked on the sound, which turned liquid and tasted like blood.

He had the knife in his hands. I knew the sound of that knife. I could feel the cold blade slide up and down my back, teasingly.

Afraid that my struggling movements might impale me, I was more afraid not to move. In one great heave I managed to turn half over and look into his face.

It was not a burglar, or the man from the mirror.
It was Patricia.

I lay in bed the next morning, having called in sick at work. My boss offered to bring me lunch. I told her I needed to be alone.

The apartment house was empty; I counted the bodies as they left, until there were none.

I listened to the rush of air in the empty walls. A musty smell washed out. The empty walls cried as the wind passed through. The sound amplified, sought itself, went round and round.

There is an emptiness here, I thought, the shells of all the lives that have filtered through the building, been contained by it. Unfelt feelings, unspoken words. And it, they, move and walk.

Over time, they seek matter and gain weight. They are like memories, a heavier infestation as the years pass.

I was full; I was empty. I wondered that I did not crash through my bed, through the floor, through the earth, never finding anything more solid than myself.

I would never stop falling.

I stubbornly got up. My legs were heavy as lead. I restlessly paced my room, knowing the value of increased gravity on the heart muscle. The quiet was slowly killing me. Which would be finished first?

I strained to hear the front door open. I could go down and get my morning newspaper. Someone would be there.

To save me.

But no one came.

I walked out the back door, down the stairs. The garbage smelled. Someone had left a lid off. I put it back on.

I sat by the pool. The landlord had cleaned out the leaves. The water smelled chokingly of chlorine. An empty pack of cigarettes, a half-full ashtray, a bottle of suntan lotion, indicated that the pool was being used.

I couldn't say who, but then, I was not looking out much anymore.

Taking off my shoes and rolling up my trousers, I dangled my feet in the cool water. Legs met legs, a wavering unsmiling face lurking near the turquoise bottom.

Hard as I tried, I could not make the unpleasant expression leave the face. It kept getting worse, drier-looking, set in stone, all downward movement and thought; a stone mask of pain buried in water.

Everything gets expressed, a friend of mind once told me; she had learned this in a mental hospital, where she had been confined as a teenager.

She told stories. An imbecilic weight lifter who walked around naked and seduced everybody. A young woman who (after she had violated some obscure rule) was carried away by the attendants, flung over their shoulders like a sack of flour. "Who needs this shit?" she shouted.

My friend thought this explained everything about life.

I heard a rustling, like windblown leaves, at the side of the house. Trying to reconstruct Linda's face (and not succeeding), I didn't turn around to look.

A gust of wind whipped around the house, shook the fences. The earth seemed to swell, a wave of earth, and the birds chattering in the tree (the half-dead palm that had set a record for size and longevity) grew still.

War?

I felt desire. Any loud noise, an unexpected wind, could mean the promised final war had finally begun. I thought about bomb shelters, fire drills, the TV movie about nuclear war that had made me sick.

The birds started up again. The wind was still. It was as if a sleeper had turned once, struggled to consciousness, then fallen back to sleep.

An earth tremor, or maybe just a truck going by out front.

I closed my eyes, thought of the moment when the walls would melt (as they must, one day), the world turning to shadows in one illuminating instant, when my thoughts would join with all the other thoughts, and we would be extinguished.

When I opened my eyes, I noted the face at the bottom of the pool had slowly begun to rise.

29

I don't know the exact moment it happened.

Patricia knocked on the window upstairs, then called down to me. She was with Paul. I was still sitting on the edge of the pool.

I waved at her over my shoulder, not bothering to turn around. I did not want her to see my face, my square face with the dark frame of hair, a face of long stretches of bone and small features, but for a large sensuous mouth.

I sat for a while longer, thought I heard the side door open again; again, I ignored it. I was busy counting the waves from my stirring feet as they broke against the far side of the pool.

Soon the pool was full of parallel lines, movement so constant that the surface looked still.

That must have been when he did it. At that moment of perfect illusion. Reached up when I wasn't looking and pulled me into the water.

I gasped for breath, but soon had turned insubstantial, into an image that didn't breathe, that could no longer move the water.

I watched him pull his feet from the pool, dry them on my towel, roll down his trousers, then stride purposefully, tensely away.

There was nothing I could do but wait.

* * *

The sun was bright. An occasional cream-colored cloud, tinted with faint pastels, floated by. I counted thirty-six such clouds; then six large formations of massed dark clouds. A line of smaller clouds, high and at first almost invisible, spread to cover the surface of the sky. They were like ripples in water, or the scales of a dragon.

I watched the sun slowly obscured and the darkness filling the sky like ink.

I had almost stopped waiting, hypnotized by the sky, when he dived into the water, and I was catapulted into the air, landing on the side of the pool.

Dry as paper.

I lingered there. Why rush into the flames? They caught up to you soon enough.

I wished he had left me in the water. The exchanges were more exhausting than surrender.

Let him have my life. I like the world better when I can't touch it.

As a duty, I walked up the back stairs. Something was in the air. There was trouble in the air. My counterpart had left a palpable trail.

When I got inside, my phone was ringing.

"Michael?" Frank said. "You sound funny, far away."

"No, Frank, I'm right here. I think this might be a bad connection." My words? Impersonal, sounding blurry even to me.

"I had to tell you," Frank continued, his voice cracking with excitement. I imagined his cheeks must be flushed. "I'm at the social worker's office, you know, the woman who was investigating Brian. Well, they've cleared me, finally. They have no doubt that it was someone else who molested him, maybe a teacher."

"Do they have any leads as to who that might be?" I asked.

"No, they say it's hard to tell. I don't know why, but they don't seem real interested in finding out. They're pretty casual about it, which makes me mad. It's like this sort of thing happens every day. Which I suppose it does."

"What's your next move?" I asked.

"I'm going to push until I find out who it was." My heart sank. "Say, Michael, have you talked to Paul Marks yet? I know you've been out-of-sorts since the street fair, but I still suspect that character had something to do with this."

I said that I hadn't, but that I would broach the subject with Paul Marks as soon as I became a coherent entity.

"One more thing . . ." Frank said as I was about to hang up. "The police have made it official, though it's what they said all along. Brian's death was an accident, an official accident." He sighed. "You know, I was starting to believe I had drowned him with my own hands."

The apartment building was waking from a long slumber. It did not wake into life, but into a waking death, having never had a life of its own. First a faint stir as unliving muscle and bone began to work together, to remember life that had passed through, had been rumored; an exhaled breath, fetid with sleep; then a low hollow growl to scare away anything that had crept up in the darkness.

The building was occupied again. I don't know why I had been worried. They come and go, and the movement never stops. They returned while I lingered poolside. Patricia, tired of the café circuit. Paul Marks, watching his video, and perhaps Janette, trysting with Fred Feretti now that Paul Marks was old news.

I stared at the phone, turned down the volume on the answering machine.

There was a sudden startling voice in the hall, running feet, the front door slamming. I couldn't tell who or what.

I waited in agony, not daring to move. Soon there was hurried activity up the stairs: like footsteps in a cave, the sound was a giant echo.

I also heard a stealthy, catlike tread on the back stairs.

I closed the windows, pulled the blinds, stood shaking in the middle of the room. Only air around me, walls of air, and I was alone.

No one was inside yet.

The doorbell rang. Though the ringing set my nerves on fire, I did not answer. Then there was a pounding on the door.

"Michael," a voice cried, so blurred with emotion that I could not tell who it was, whether it was male or female. "Michael, if you're in there, please answer."

I stood frozen. I could feel the other one moving behind the curtains, under the blinds, in the shiny surfaces of the tables, on the polished floors (if I dared look down; I did not).

Outside, more voices, official-sounding voices, strong, urgent. They had come up the stairs in a stampede.

"When did you find her?"

"Just now," the unidentified voice said. Intense emotions made all voices alike. "She was there, lying half in, half out of the apartment. The door was open."

Which apartment? I was burning with equal desire to know and not to know.

"Is she dead?"

"I'm sorry."

I packed my suitcase and waited by the back door until I was sure I wouldn't be seen.

I padded down the back stairs, made my way past the swimming pool, casting an accusing glance at the still water.

No one looked out the windows. They were all in the lobby.

There was a door behind the gazebo which led into the alley.

I had parked two feet into a crosswalk. If you didn't get home by ten o'clock, there were no legal spaces left to park.

Everyone went to bed early now, like good little children. I pulled the ticket from the windshield, tore it in two, and threw it into the wind.

Getting into the car, I warmed the motor for five minutes, then drove away.

The cabin where I was headed belonged to Dorothy and me. We had not agreed on who should take it, so we still held joint custody. Consequently, it was never used.

I waited impatiently at the entrance to the bridge. Traffic was lined up for half a mile. An accident? Or one of those masses of people that seem to come from nowhere, then disappear in the blink of an eye?

San Francisco was a moody city, either filled to bursting or desolate; I had not learned to predict when or understand why. Moods were like weather; best come prepared for anything.

Today the whole city seemed to be going over the bridge with me. We were all escaping from something. The thought made me feel good. One person to a car, faces pointed straight ahead, not even a quick glance into the rearview mirror.

If you didn't know this was real, you would think you were paranoid.

Finally the traffic started to move, like blood washing away a clot. The feeling of freedom as the traffic suddenly took off, like a flock of startled birds, was orgasmic.

I shot into the middle lane. The clouds, whose passage I had observed while underwater, had congealed into a solid mass, stretching around the neck of the Bay like a shroud. The white-capped water was mercury-colored; a massive gray tanker moved toward the bridge, followed by several smaller boats.

I waited for the exhilaration I always felt when I reached the other side of the bridge. But a thick anxiety filled my chest instead.

I turned on the radio. The traffic was still heavy, and it seemed everyone was angry. Yes, this was one of those days. Everyone was in a bad mood, a bad place, like me.

A black BMW cut me off, for no good reason. I hit the brakes.

As revenge (the BMW was soon out of sight), I tailgated a slow-moving car covered with bumper stickers: "Save Mono Lake," "Question Authority," "A Nuclear Bomb Could Ruin Your Whole Day." A "Child on Board" sign swayed in the back window.

I honked, motioned him to the right lane, but he wouldn't budge. In fact, he slowed even more.

As I passed, I noticed that the driver, behind closed windows, was singing. Trapped in his own world. Yet something had made him slow when I had urged him on, an instinctive perversity. I honked again as I passed, but he did not acknowledge me.

The clouds were slowly clearing as I traveled north. In the rearview mirror I could see them still hovering over the city, like smoke from a mammoth fire.

The road wound through massed boulders that seemed on the verge of tumbling down, up an incline so faint that only the whining of the engine told of its presence, and then onto a flat brown plain. It didn't take long for the plants to die after the dry season had started. Black barns in the distance, cut through with sunlight, mottled cattle standing on shadow-and-sun-dappled hillsides, horses grazing in cool blue hollows.

When would the gravity of the city let me go? Today the backward pull was heavy. As I traveled forward, the temptation to return seemed to grow, as though I were attached by a cord that could be stretched only so far, and then would snap back.

The freeway narrowed to two lanes; I pulled into the center lane and tried to dispel the inertia. Speed would do it, if nothing else. I was ahistorical; nothing could touch me as long as I moved.

I pushed down the pedal further and further. A small thing really, but after a while it helped. The car would save me.

The land got tawny, faintly rolling, barbed-wire fences right down to the road. I wondered that anyone would bother with the expense; anyway, there were holes that any clever child could get through.

I bet there aren't many who would try to get to that barren land.

Eventually the land smoothed out; the only hills were well off the road and could have been clouds hugging the horizon.

When I passed Santa Rosa, I began to feel a little better.

I opened the window. Smoke, diesel oil, manure, rubber heated by asphalt.

Satisfied that I had escaped—at least for now—I settled into the drive.

An hour and a half later, I turned off the freeway onto Black Mountain Road.

Dorothy and I had liked the spookiness of the name. We joked about evil doings in the woods. It was easy to imagine anything up here; there was a special darkness under the massive redwoods. The shadows had shape, and seemed to spread outward to cover the land as the sun set.

Two years before Dorothy and I separated, a make-shift grave had been found nearby, filled with the skeletons of young boys. Carved on a tree, in the center of a heart, were the words "The Lightning Man." The authorities supposed this was the killer identifying himself poetically.

They never found the man. They identified a few of the boys, some of whom were runaways of the sort that always flock to the Bay. How do you reconstruct a human life from bones?

Some of the bones had been there for ten years, others

only two. They buried the unidentified remains in an un-marked grave.

The authorities guessed that whoever the man was, he had moved on to greener pastures. Or had merely grown tired; or satisfied.

A comfortable retirement from murder.

Dorothy felt strange after hearing about the deaths, al-though it was old news, even then. She kept the cabin door locked. I told her she was being silly, the man was probably six states away, or dead. Also, she was not a tender young boy.

We came to the country to feel free, not to be afraid.

When I returned from my usual twilight walks in the redwoods, Dorothy's face was anxious and strained; like cardboard that has been rained on, then dried.

I suggested she come with me, though I didn't really want her to.

It was my special private time. I loved watching the sun as it twisted out of the sky, setting behind the trees, now green-black, then black with silver lights that had once been leaves, then dark as the sky itself. You could almost hear the land falling asleep, the slow breath, the sinking into self and dream.

I guessed she knew how I felt, because she never accom-panied me on my evening walks.

After a while she began to find reasons not to come up to the cabin on weekends.

I turned onto a narrow paved road, then a dirt road badly in need of repair. Clouds of white dust rose up. I was thrown about in my seat, my head bumped the roof and I cursed. The shocks were gone. Metal ground on metal, there was a sickening thud as though something would fall out, but in the final moments did not.

I had not been to the cabin since one weekend right after the divorce, when I sat dry-eyed on the porch and watched the empty lane.

The cabin appeared through the trees, like a window in the air you did not see being thrown open. You turned and something that was not there suddenly was full and complete.

Even from a distance I could see the dust that covered the cabin like a veil, the crooked windows, the sagging porch, like the bowed back of a tired animal.

30

didn't go in right away.

I parked the car and started the once-familiar walk to the redwood forest. There were no other houses on the road. The back of our property looked onto bare acreage with a single run-down barn. Sunlight filtered through the broken boards, turning the adjacent field into a patchwork quilt, which shimmered as the wind blew the loose boards about. They creaked in the wind like a chorus of crickets.

I moved down the chalky lane, past the field, around the bend, where the forest appeared like a sudden summer storm in another land.

I had come this way so often, in a somewhat happier time. Some pieces of that light-filled man must remain in the lane, in that beam of sunlight, or in the pungent smell my feet raised as I entered the cool forest, a spirit waiting to be reunited with its host.

But I found no hint of him, of the man I was. I kept walking.

I found the small hollow where I used to sit and imagine that I was a child again, hiding from Mother.

I sat down. The ground was unpleasantly rough, the lichen brown and hard. When I got up, my pants were damp.

I looked up, spun around, imagining that I was still and the treetops whirled.

There was a stone well deeper in the forest. Maybe that would shake some feelings loose. It might still have water.

Though in the deep-summer months it sometimes dried out. I began a brisk walk toward it. I took off my shirt. The sunlight that fell in long poles through the trees struck my chest and I felt a little refreshed.

I started to run. Dark to light, light to dark.

My blood rushed. I felt like a forest animal. A cloudy warm feeling spread through my body.

I ran without thinking. It was like losing myself.

Suddenly I stopped. I had gone deep into the forest. I felt eyes watching me. The forest was now smothering, threatening. The trees surrounded me like apparitions of men that might come alive, tall, dark, stalking men, with clubs in their hands.

When I looked over my shoulder, I thought I saw one of them rise up—a tall tree-straight man—and duck behind the other trees.

I started up again. Leaves rustled, a thin wind moved down the lane. I could feel him in my head, like a heart-beat, though I did not look at him directly. That would give him power.

When I went round a bend, I glanced back in a motion that I hoped looked like a natural part of running, to see him become a tree, or the shadow of a tree.

I ran under a gray peeling branch. It looked like it had eczema. My head struck the branch. I cried out. Slowing for an instant, I gave the branch a savage blow; it broke off dryly, fell to the ground.

I was soaking wet and panting like a hunted animal. I couldn't tell how far I had come. I looked over my shoulder. No sign of pursuit.

Apparently I had outrun him.

I sat down, brushed twigs from my legs. When I looked up, I saw that I had reached my destination. I remembered the well as a deep stone basin filled with dark water that had seemed bottomless. You could tell your fortune in the deep water. People sometimes threw in coins.

I had to look twice to realize the shallow stone hole was what I had sought.

Moving behind the well, I squatted so that I was half out of sight. You could never be too careful. A couple of inches of green scummy water covered the bottom of the well. Water spiders played across the surface.

I put a finger in the water, which easily touched bottom.

A small animal had been living inside the cabin. I stood in the door, key in hand. There were black droppings all over the floor. The old green couch where Dorothy and I used to lie and watch night fall had been his bed.

I threw open the windows; the wood was dry and soft, and the putty around the glass almost gone. The panes rattled but did not fall out.

There was an inch of dust on the floor. I found the broom in the broom closet, and cleaning stuff under the sink. Everything was just as we had left it; I was reminded of *The Time Machine* when the protagonist visited his house in the future.

But I had to sleep somewhere, so I kept cleaning.

There was a hornet's nest in the backyard, next to the pump. I closed the window facing the nest.

After two hours the cabin was livable, for a night at least.

The sun moved from front to back; the shadows lengthened behind me. I changed into shorts and sandals.

I cleaned the bird droppings from the white metal chair on the front porch. Sitting down, I tried to imagine Dorothy coming down the lane, brightness folding itself out of the trees. Her brisk walk, eyes to the ground, not downcast, but looking.

She had collected rocks, twigs, things that clung to the earth.

Brown hair that turned almost blond in the summer, lank shiny hair like a boy's. She was forever brushing it out of her eyes.

But there was only wind in the lane.

I searched, but my heart, though many-chambered, felt dry, a faint rub in my chest.

The first time we seriously spoke of it was our first summer here. The conversation had been gentle, probing, agreeable. The second summer, the trouble began. Yes, we would have children, I said, but she wanted to know when, in a year, two, five? She liked to plan ahead. When she talked about it, her eyes turned glassy and remote, and she looked at me as if I didn't exist.

Some part of my heart closed up that second summer. Hers, as well. Year after year the process continued.

At the end, the demands became feverish. I had always loved the way she looked at me, so that I saw myself differently, almost as much as I loved her for who she was.

Slowly I shrank in her sight.

When the demands about having a family interfered with this way of seeing, I grew stubborn.

And so Dorothy blinded herself to me; and gave me up.

I looked down at my hands. I had been clutching the railing so tightly that a splinter of wood had lodged in my palm. I tried to remove it, but a piece of it had gone too deep.

The sun fell to the treetops. The leaves went black, and when the wind shivered, they shivered whitely, then turned black again.

I went back inside, and brooded in the darkness, breathing in the dust and letting the feeling of emptiness grow.

Maybe it would reach clear down to the hurt.

I put the sleeping bag on the bare springs of the four-poster bed. The bed was almost as big as the room; Dorothy's idea. The bed had belonged to her grandmother. I had found the mattress in the garage, green wth mold and crawling inside. A fine nesting place for insects.

It was a warm night, and there were stars, milky clouds of them.

I rolled over in the down sleeping bag, a little unnerved that I was not home in bed. I had not slept anywhere but in my own bed for months. Could it have been years? There was something terrifying about falling asleep in a strange place.

When I closed my eyes, I tried to imagine that I was safe. I could not. The insects were screaming in the yard, the wind moaned like no city wind. I gave up trying. I concentrated on the feeling of the springs against my back.

The sensation was not unpleasant, small circular burnings all over my back and buttocks and legs, like tiny fingers pressed into my flesh.

I fell asleep facing the wooden wall.

Something woke me. My heart jumped but I remained still.

I turned over, opened my eyes. Someone stood at the foot of my bed.

"I'll close the window," the soft voice said. "It's cold. I didn't mean to wake you."

She wore a towel wrapped about her waist. Her breasts were bare, gleaming with water. The nipples were black in the moonlight.

She walked slowly to the window, her hips swiveling.

"I'll go back to sleep, Mother," I said, pressing my face into the fragant pillows.

As she left, she leaned over and kissed me. A firm smooth breast grazed my arm, burning like fire.

I got up and looked out the window. It was fall; you could see the leaves littering the ground, black and white in the light of an almost full moon. Recently stripped branches rubbed and stirred as the wind passed through them; and from far away, the howl of a wolf, the hooting of an owl.

There was the pump where we got water, my bicycle

(which I had convinced Father to let me bring; it had rattled on top of the car all during the fourteen-hour drive), the boat that tomorrow we would take down to the water.

I went back to bed. When morning came, Father left in a hurry, to go across to the mainland to get some things he needed for the boat.

When I went into the bathroom to brush my teeth, Mother was sitting in the big claw-footed bathtub.

I was embarrassed; a new feeling when I saw her naked.

"Come get in with me," she said. "Why waste the water?"

I hesitated. "I can wait," I said.

"Oh, don't be silly. We used to take baths together all the time. You're still a little boy."

I let my robe drop and climbed into the deep blue water. Mother washed my back, shampooed my hair. I stared at the water as it grew scummy with soap.

The front door of the cabin opened. Mother looked startled, started to get up.

Father stood in the doorway, a black shape, slowly moving forward.

I huddled low, choked on water. Mother had covered herself with a violet towel.

"Honey, I thought you were gone for the morning," she said sweetly, and kissed him. He didn't seem to notice the kiss, but was boring holes in me with his eyes.

Mother disappeared into the bedroom. Father came forward, leaned down, his eyes staring at the drain. He grabbed my hair, pushed me roughly against the back of the tub, and then, hesitating only a moment, pushed me under.

I clawed at him with my hands. My eyes were open and I could see the devil-red face and that hairy hand holding me down.

Mother had come back in and was screaming at Father to stop.

But she did not come forward. She did not use her body to stop him.

When I thought my lungs would burst, he let me up for a moment. I gasped burning air, then was underwater again.

Mother was still screaming somewhere in the distance.

He dunked me again and again, letting me catch a breath just before my lungs would burst.

When he stopped, I was as limp as a rag, sobbing tiredly. He pushed roughly past Mother and slammed out the front door.

Mother came over and put her arm around me. But I shrugged her off.

"Leave me alone," I cried. "You're as bad as he is."

The sun had come up; birds were rustling in the underbrush outside the window.

I got dressed, tried to ignore my rumbling stomach. I couldn't stay here. Who knew what would find me?

Yet it was daylight and there was one more thing I wanted to do.

I hurried down the path to the redwood forest, but took an adjoining path that skirted the forest rather than the one that went through. Trees saw everything; too much; even thoughts, half-formed desires.

In about fifteen minutes I came to a clearing behind a barn long abandoned even in those early years.

This was where they had found the graves of the young boys. The remains had been removed after their discovery.

I had come here often, when dark feelings overtook me, more so in the later years as Dorothy became a stranger, then dead to me.

In my imagination, I would overturn the earth and throw another body onto the pile: the body of a child I had killed, in fantasy, on the walk here.

Today, no fantasy came. I stood in the purple shadow of the barn, strips of sunlight moving on the ground now covered with grass and tall weeds, some with unlikely flowers.

No pain, no tears, no grief; just the shape of a small boy in my heart, strongly outlined, empty inside, always calling for more.

I turned around and ran back up the path to the cabin. I left the door unlocked, and started the car.

Maybe there was a chance; maybe I could fill up that space, finally. But not here.

I had to go back to the city.

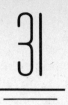

I crept into the building.

The place smelled different, like new paint or carpet, though that didn't seem likely; the landlord didn't do anything unless the tenants signed a petition.

The apartment doors were closed. No lights inside, just the halo of fluorescent fixtures in the hallway that usually made my skin look splotchy. Today my skin looked perfect, poreless, a strangely uniform color, like android skin.

There was a note pinned to my door. I stuffed it in my pocket without reading it. Someone had piled my newspapers in front of my door. I picked them up and hurried inside.

The clock said it was a little past noon. It was Monday. I called my boss and told her I had the stomach flu, that I hadn't been able to make it to the phone till now. My voice didn't sound convincing—too smooth, not the voice of a man who had spent the last several hours with his face in the toilet.

My boss accepted what I said without question; I felt a little elated as I hung up the receiver.

I opened a window, glanced down at the pool. Free of leaves, lit by the noonday sun, it was like a clear glass eye, blue and featureless.

I couldn't resist its stare. I slipped into my Speedos and ran down the back stairs.

As I dived in, a thought flickered through me: Someone is dead. You have to find out who.

I did thirty laps, pushing myself hard, feeling every muscle of my body contract and release, swimming underwater every other length.

As I came up for air on the thirty-first lap, a hand reached down and touched my shoulder, a rough hand.

I remembered when I had been trapped underwater looking up at myself. I thought it had happened again. But I was wrong.

There was a real person standing there, changed almost beyond recognition.

It was Paul Marks.

"Paul," I said shyly, pulling myself from the pool in one agile motion, "what's up?"

At first he didn't reply. Then in a gravelly voice, as though he had a bad cold, he said, "Michael, where have you been? Everyone's been looking for you."

I stared at him. He seemed smaller, perhaps because the smooth terrain of his skin now had details, an infinite number of details.

There were blue circles under his eyes, his perfect nose now showed a bump in the center where it apparently had been broken, his hair was cut badly so that the tops of his ears, which protruded, were visible, and he had scars on both wrists, white against the tanned skin (suicide gesture or carpal-tunnel surgery?).

"I've been away for a day or two. Up north," I said, enjoying his distress, which I could feel swelling like a wave. I realized for the first time how much I hated him.

"There's been some bad business while you were gone. Very bad." Around his knees were webs of scars, pulling into the underlying tissues when he moved; I guessed old sports injuries.

What had brought perfect Paul's imperfections to the surface with such force?

I traced the scars like a map, not bothering to hide my

attention, and enjoyed the journey immensely. He was wearing cutoffs. I wondered at his lack of pride, which had seemed his most salient feature.

I continued toweling dry.

Paul put his hand on my shoulder. The palm was cracked, callused, unlike the fleshy, silken palm that had pinned me to his bed.

"Don't you care?" he asked, his voice cracking.

"Care about what?" I asked, pretending not to have apprehension. The clear cool water had emptied me of all residual feeling.

"Janette," he said. "Janette is dead."

A soft knock on the door. I was staring at the new curtain I had thrown over the mirror, a sheet I used to sunbathe on. It was stained with coconut butter.

"Coming," I said, getting up slowly. I walked to the door, one step for each heartbeat.

I had barely unhooked the chain when the door burst open and Patricia was inside. Her face was red, squinting like a child's after it has cried all night.

She threw herself into my arms without looking at me.

Now that I'm getting taller and darker, I thought quite illogically, she finds me attractive again.

I put my arms around her dumbly, closed the circle with my clasped hands at her back, and waited. No feelings; a reflex action; what was expected. If she were looking for feeling, then she could try to get it from Paul, I thought, and with as much success.

She sobbed into my shirt. The dampness soaked through to my skin: cold and clammy. I put a hand under her chin and elevated her face, a gesture drawn from sentimental movies.

She looked up with surprise. "Michael?" she asked. I nodded.

I walked her into the sunlit living room. "My eyes are playing tricks on me," she said, then sat down heavily. "At first I thought . . ."

I stood staring at her from the center of the room. "Patricia, calm down. It's awful, I know. Awful." As I said the word a second time, I almost felt it; but the feeling was ghostlike, pulled through me like chains; then it disappeared through an inner wall.

Patricia seemed out of focus, not herself at all. The tidal blur of emotions made her that way. Suddenly she pulled herself upright, assumed the posture I had learned to recognize as Patricia.

"Michael," she said, firmly, "where have you been? We've been looking all over for you. Actually, waiting mostly. I don't know much about your life outside the building. We didn't know where to look."

"I was up north. An impulse took over and I just hit the road. Bad timing, I guess." I sat down across from her, leaned forward across the coffee table. "But in a way I'm glad I was gone. I don't know if I could have stood it."

Patricia's face softened. The look of accusation that was forming melted. A single tear traced a silver line down her cheek, a slow sinuous motion.

She looked tired. Her full eyes had dark rings about them. Her hair hung in strings, going in many different directions at once.

"It's been a nightmare," she said. "You can't know. I haven't slept since it happened. No one is safe. No one."

"I know what you mean," I said. "If Janette can die, then what's in store for the rest of us?"

"A strange distracted sort of survival, I would guess," Patricia said. She stared at the ceiling. "I feel half-dead myself. I don't think I'll ever be the same."

"Me either."

We didn't say anything for a while. We stared at each other's hands. Mine were still; hers were pale and trembling.

The sun moved through the yard, brightening the edges of the leaves outside the window, darkening the centers. After a while they looked like negatives of leaves.

"There's more to it," Patricia said, out of the blue. "I have suspicions."

"Suspicions?" I asked, not sure I wanted to know.

"The police don't know who's responsible. They seem to think it was a one-night stand, the Mr. Goodbar type of thing. But I know better. Janette said it herself when we found Brian. Something stinks in this building. Whatever responsibility there is, lies here." She pointed to the ceiling, to the floor, to the walls.

I glanced nervously at my shrouded mirror.

"Paul Marks ..." she said, and stopped. The name just stood there, like a diver on the edge of a cliff.

"I thought you and he had gotten close," I said.

"No, not really. Well, at first I thought maybe ... Also, I was sleuthing, at Frank's request. We didn't dare tell you anything, because you've been so weird lately. We thought you might tell Janette and she would tell Paul—and then we'd have found out nothing," she said.

"I just saw him out back," I said, trying to keep the satisfaction out of my voice. "He looked awful."

"Well, this has really worn on him. I mean really. You can almost see the guilt ooze out of him. He is all scars now, all sewn together. The monster has risen to the surface." She bit her lip, as though not sure if she wanted to continue.

"The spiritual disintegration of the modern man," I said, trying to keep the conversation intellectual.

"You know, the knife that killed Janette was your knife. I told the police I had seen it in Janette's apartment the night before the murder, so you're off the hook. With that ornate handle it's hard to miss. But I didn't see it in Janette's apartment—I saw it in Paul's apartment, next to his bed, a few hours before Janette was killed." She looked at me questioningly.

"I don't know how it got there," I said. "A lot of my stuff has made its way upstairs lately."

"Margaret was also at the police station. She staunchly defended you. She was acting strong, but I could see the pain underneath. You know, I think she really loved Janette, the real Janette, the one we didn't get to know."

I kept quiet.

"There's more," Patricia said, wiping away tears. "Janette told me that you sometimes climbed up on the balcony and watched her and Paul together. I mean, after the first time."

My face filled with blood, and my mouth swelled shut.

"Don't look that way. We're all crazy. And she told me another thing, something she had just found out a week or two ago. Paul had a potency problem. His penis would not get erect. Missing some sort of triggering nerve or something. Anyway, he had an implant, a sort of balloon that blows up when he pushes his groin; there is a small pump buried there."

I remembered the peculiar pumping motion when Paul Marks rose to full height; I repressed a smile.

"Janette was leafing through some papers in Paul's desk. He found her looking at surgical bills, which spelled out pretty clearly what the procedure was. Janette was no dummy—she had seen the PBS special about the implants. When she confronted Paul with it, he freaked. Threw her out. I could hear him screaming at her in the hall. *Screaming.*"

"So you think—"

"That he did it, out of revenge, or to keep her quiet. But Janette had already spilled the beans to me. And in a not-very-kind way. I felt sorry for Paul, a little. It's not an easy thing for a man to admit he's impotent."

I pretended to muse on that.

"And there's another thing," she said. She was wringing her hands like mad. "I have a friend at the police station, a clerk who is someone I've acted with before. He let me into the precinct the other night when it was almost empty. I took the knife that Janette was killed with."

My mouth fell open.

"I couldn't stop myself. It was a compulsion. I knew it was wrong, and if they find out, they'll think I had something to do with the killing. But I couldn't stand to think of your knife there in that plastic bag, with Janette's blood all over it."

The color drained from her face. She looked at me sheepishly, as though asking for approval.

"Where is it now?" I asked.

"In my apartment."

32

The police questioned me.

I was not sure what to think; so I didn't attempt to put it into words, even to myself. Would they have believed me if I had said I'd been underwater when the deed was done?

They had no reason to suspect me, although they questioned me extensively about the knife. They spoke of it as though it were a fetish object, or a criminal itself. I told them I had picked the knife up at a garage sale; that I used it to cut cheese; that Janette often borrowed things without asking; that the handle looked like onyx but probably wasn't. Patricia's story about having seen the knife confirmed my story. Frank had apparently not mentioned seeing the knife on my bedstand; perhaps he did not associate the murder weapon with that knife. He was not terribly observant.

My trip out of town was the object of mild suspicion; but when I told them I had gone to the cabin where my ex-wife and I had spent a great deal of time, one of the officers, the short Irish one, also divorced, said he understood.

Sometimes you needed to remember pain so that you could get rid of it.

No pantomime, just a perfect understanding.

He looked at me and I looked at him. I didn't know him

and he didn't know me. That was the nature of our under-standing.

I raised my hand, bringing him forward.

He stepped out of the mirror, moved toward me. His lips brushed mine.

He turned away, walked to the window.

He went to the living room and turned on the TV too loud. He got a beer from the refrigerator. He propped his feet on the coffee table. He belched.

For an hour there were two of us, bumping into things, fighting over chairs, television stations, when we would go see Patricia, should we ask for the knife.

"Do you think the police will be back?" I asked.

"Sure, they suspect everyone. It's their job until they find out who did it. Though I don't think in this case they ever will."

"What do you mean by that?" I asked, irritated by the innuendo.

"I mean some mysteries are supposed to stay unsolved. Are not solvable, in a real sense."

"So you're not going to tell me what part you—we—played in these various goings-on."

"That's exactly right," he said.

Frank had gotten mildly drunk. He was crying one min-ute, dry and starey-eyed the next. He and Janette had not been the best of friends, but Frank was a softhearted sort, and I'm sure this reminded him of Brian's death as well.

If he hadn't cared that much for either of them, then the tears seemed wasted to me, though I didn't say so.

"You sure seem calm," Frank said in one of his dry pe-riods. "I thought you and Janette were thick as thieves."

"Not lately," I said tersely. "Oh, I didn't mean that. I'm upset, of course I'm upset." I let my voice rise, to show him I meant it. "It's just that when I'm really upset, I get deadly calm. A trait I inherited from my father."

I heard footsteps on the stairway, halting, then rushing forward. From the weight of the steps, I guessed Paul Marks, though the tempo was off. Then I reminded myself that Paul Marks was a changed man, no longer possessed of perfect timing. This new lurching gait might well signify the latest transformation of the monster.

I went to the door, looked out. It was Paul, ragged as a tree shadow flying apart in wind.

He rushed up the stairs to his apartment, walked heavily to his bed, and sat down (two thumps on the ceiling must have been his shoes dropping).

Frank was reading a newspaper, looking tired and care-worn. I felt sorry for him. He was a decent man, a generous spirit. He could not begin to understand the complex unfoldings of the last several months.

I went to the balcony, looked down into the yard at the pool: the backside of the place where I lived, not a home, just somewhere to be, to pass time.

Paul Marks was moving about, dragging his feet like chains. I followed him from the bedroom to the living room, to the kitchen, and then into the bathroom.

Frank looked up. "Michael, what are you doing, pacing around like that? You look like a caged animal."

"I feel like I'm about ready to jump out of my skin," I said; then shivered.

There were footsteps in the hallway, faint, firm, the ringing of a doorbell.

Why was Patricia going into Paul Marks's apartment, if she suspected what she did?

I felt a lancing apprehension, barely stopped myself from rushing into the hall. Instead, I sat down next to Frank and waited.

The wait wasn't long. Within fifteen minutes of relatively tense quiet the uproar began, like an earthquake. There were strange strangled voices, seemingly neither male nor female.

Thundering feet, doors slamming, things crashing to the door.

Frank looked at me. "Hey, what's going on up there?" he said to the ceiling.

When the noise continued to rise, his expression grew concerned and he stood up.

"Maybe we should go up and see if there's a problem," he said.

"Oh, maybe it's just—" I said, when I heard, felt, in the middle of my spine, as though it emanated from my own nervous system, a single sustained scream that shook the walls, and sent Frank and me racing into the hall.

We ran up the stairs. Patricia was stumbling out of Paul Marks's apartment, holding the bloody knife in her hands.

"I was showing it to him, accusing him with it," she babbled, tears flooding her face.

"Call an ambulance," she said, and dropped the knife.

33

When they put Paul Marks on the stretcher, they pulled his hands away from his groin. The wound looked like a rosebud opened before its time.

Paul twisted in agony, bloodying the sheets. I could not take my eyes off him. He seemed to shrink as the blood fountained from the ruptured prosthesis. There were lines rising all over his skin, as the vitality poured out, puckered scars that made him look like a badly sewn leather jacket.

Frank grabbed my elbow. I stood completely still, all eyes.

"Come on," he said. "They'll take care of it," meaning the medics. I looked them over: two well-muscled gay men in immaculate white uniforms. They seemed to know what they were doing.

Their smooth tan faces betrayed no sign that the nature of the wound disturbed them.

I allowed myself to be pulled toward Patricia's apartment, where a short black policeman was talking softly to the door.

"Open up, young lady. You'll only make matters worse."

I could hear Patricia sobbing wildly, a scattered sound that seemed a mixture of stunned hilarity and incomprehensible grief.

"Let me try," I said. "I'm a friend."

"Okay," he said with a slight edge of territoriality in his

voice, "see what you can do. If not, we'll have to break it down."

"Patricia," I said, "this is Michael." I tried to keep my voice even, warm. It sounded strange even to me.

In between sobs I could hear, "Michael?" as though she did not believe me; as though she had forgotten who I was, but wanted to believe.

"Michael," I said firmly. "Open up. You've got to face the music, now or later. The landlord will get real cranky if the door has to be broken down."

Frank looked at me in horror.

"This is no joking matter," he said, and pushed me away. "Patricia, come out now." That was all, simply, authoritatively.

The door opened.

She came into the light, skin mottled, her eyes all but swollen shut, black streaks running down her cheeks like paint.

"He tried to rape me," she said, her voice regaining composure. She wiped at her cheek, looked at her black-and-bloody hand in horror.

"He tried to rape me," she repeated, "and so I let the air out of it—out of him." She paused, laughed a brief horrible laugh, looking at each of our faces, as if to see whether we were capable of understanding.

"But I didn't find out what I wanted to know. I still don't know who is guilty. And of what." She brushed past me unseeing. Frank reached out to her, but she shrugged off his hand.

"Take me to the police station," she said. "I'm ready to tell my story."

The police wouldn't let us ride with them. I was glad. I told Frank I wanted to go upstairs for a few minutes and pull myself together.

Instead, when the car had driven away, and Frank had gone back to his apartment to get his coat, I walked across the street into the schoolyard that looked down on our building.

All the lights were on. I imagined insects buzzing, chattering. Shadows moved back and forth across drawn shades, ceaselessly. The appearance of life, but a strange absence of substance.

I tried to remember the discomfort I had felt on moving in—displaced, distracted, scarcely human—but I could not even elicit a dull ache this night.

The building seemed to call me, but in a voice directed away from, not toward me. I could hear its call only by the echo, hollowed by some distant unseen wall.

From my throat came a dry answer, like the scratching of feet across floors, the legs of insects, the settling of the building in the night while its inhabitants slept a dead sleep, casting for dreams in a dry well.

I walked across the street and inside. My kingdom. The musty smell, like old clothes you find in the attic, the stairway that wound from floor to floor under a dirty skylight, cracked and taped with silver tape.

Frank called down. "I'm ready," he said.

I cringed. I could feel the emotion in his voice, like unwashed skin.

I didn't know where we should go: hospital or police station?

I would have preferred the hospital. I imagined that someone had called Paul's sister and she would be there, full of grief and questions. In her distressed state, she might blurt out some of her real relationship with her brother.

Patricia would probably be questioned all night long. Was there any sense in waiting in a dim blue room on uncomfortable plastic chairs?

In a state of indifferent autonomy, I walked up the stairs. I couldn't tell Frank how I felt, what I wanted.

"Okay, Frank," I said, "you lead the way." Though what I meant to say was: You lead the way—for now.

Though I think Frank saw something in my eyes. Because he turned away when he looked at me, quickly, not saying a word.

And that was not like Frank.

That was like me.

Frank drove silently. He stared straight ahead, as you might when you have picked up a suspicious hitchhiker.

"Where are we going?" I asked finally.

"To the police station," he said.

We pulled into Mission Station. A red Cadillac with a sign in the back window that said "Ex-Boyfriend in Trunk" pulled in in front of us, slowed to a halt. Frank honked.

Frank pulled into a parking place, grumbling. He got out. I started to follow him. He motioned me to stay still.

There was a sea of black-and-white police cars in the parking lot, but a strange lack of activity. I huddled in the seat, watching, waiting. The red Cadillac was still half-blocking the driveway. A frowsy blond stood by the passenger door and pulled out a man so drunk that he looked to be made of rubber. She would prop him onto her shoulder, and he would slide off; then she'd start up again.

In a couple of minutes Frank came back with a sour look on his face.

"She's not here," he said. "They took her downtown so she could talk to some detectives. This place is empty, only one cop on duty and a clerk, who was drunk."

Without saying another word, he got in and started up. I relaxed into the seat. I closed my eyes and imagined I was part of the seat.

In no time, we were there.

"I don't think they believed me," Patricia said in the foyer of the emergency room. "But they decided not to hold me tonight, which is something. God, the place was awful. Not like you'd imagine. Just dead-feeling. Like an empty bunker, but with bored people asking you questions you knew they had asked a million times before."

"You seem pretty calm," Frank said, putting his arm around Patricia.

"The doctor gave me some Valium." She pointed to the window where a plump faced nurse filled out forms. An ambulance had just pulled up and there was a scurry of activity in the rear as they prepared for the next attack.

The police had suggested we take Patricia to San Francisco General. We went to Franklin Medical Center instead: a concrete block with shining eyes, but very efficient, and seldom crowded. The police had said that although it was only attempted rape, she should be looked over.

"The doctor checked the bruises on my arm," Patricia said, "and asked me if I felt all right. He had a copy of the police report. He looked at me strangely. I guess he didn't like what I did."

"Patricia," Frank said, "when you go for the gold, you don't mess around."

"Maybe we should check on Paul," I said, my voice filled with pity and hostility. "I asked at the front desk and they said he's back from surgery."

"How convenient my adversary and I are being healed at the same hospital," Patricia said. She had washed her face. Without makeup, and with the Valium softening her features, she looked beautiful.

We walked out into the circular driveway. The stretcher was being pulled out of the ambulance. I walked by, and caught a glimpse of a face. Balding, scared eyes, the left side of his face frozen. He had a hopeless look, as though he had been expecting this for a long time.

"He's lost himself too," I said under my breath.

"Huh?" Frank said. He held Patricia like a protective father. I felt left out and stifled a feeling of resentment.

"You guys go home," I said. "I'll take a bus back. My curiosity has gotten the better of me. I've got to go check on Paul Marks."

Before they could protest, I had ducked back into the bright shadow of the hospital.

* * *

"Visiting hours are over," the man at the front desk said finally.

"He's family," I said, forcing out a tear. "Please, he called me on the phone. He sounded so alone, so afraid. Couldn't I go up just for a few minutes?"

The man's hard face softened, melted into a blue mass, sentimental, nonspecific. I steadied myself, remembering that my tears were not real.

"Okay," he said, looking around furtively. "You go on, but be quick about it. Rules are rules."

Rules are made to be broken, I thought, and punched the elevator button.

There was no one at the nurse's station. I went directly to Paul's room. His sister was sleeping on a lime-green bench outside the room, dead to the world. She looked like a rumpled grocery bag.

I walked carefully past her, pushed open the blue door that looked thick and heavy but was surprisingly light. Either good hinges or a false center.

Paul was invisible beneath heaped white blankets, white as snow.

There were lines of clear fluid running from shining bottles, a machine at the head of his bed blinking green digital numbers.

I felt suddenly heavy, stricken, and sat down. There was a small window that looked out onto a dark field, where I knew, in the daylight, children played, people sunbathed; at night, there were sharp shadows with dogs, and sharper shadows carrying televisions on their backs, and other stolen goods.

I looked out the window into the sullen night, trying to ignore what I had come to see.

Suddenly Paul moaned. A muffled cry, like a child dreaming of drowning or waking and finding himself turned around under the covers and unable to get out.

I closed my eyes and felt the room fill with water.

I opened my eyes.

Paul had stopped breathing. I could feel it in the center

of my chest: a palpable stillness. A light was flashing on the console above the bed. Soon the room would be full of people.

I had to have one last look. Quickly I pulled the covers back.

He was small, shrunken like a mummy, pores as big as the heads of pins, each moment of his unlived life written on his skin in scars. Where he had once held his pride, there was now a swatch of cloth, white, tattered, covering nothing.

Hearing voices, I opened the door.

"Help," I said faintly. "Something's wrong."

I walked outside as the people in white sailed past me, into the room where the dead man lay.

Paul's sister had wakened, bolted upright.

She looked at me as though she were dreaming. A look of diffuse seduction passed across her eyes, then surprise.

"What are you doing up?" she asked; and then, "Who are you?"

"A close friend," I said. She went into the room, and I heard a sharp cry.

I walked to the end of the corridor, pressed my face against the cold blank glass.

I was in a room filled with water. The water drove the air from my lungs; filled my veins, washed out the final heat. My ears were crashing with the sound of water rushing over stones.

Standing there, feeling the death around me like a benefactor, I drowned.

34

I didn't sleep that night. I sat staring at the ceiling, listening and waiting.

Frank called me in the morning.

"Michael," he said solemnly, "I just found out that Paul Marks died last night."

"I know," I said. "I was there." I didn't even try to fill my voice with feeling.

"Why didn't you come up and tell us?" Frank sounded angry. "Patricia and I were up all night, waiting. We didn't hear you come in."

"I wasn't in the mood to see anyone. I needed to be alone."

"*You* needed to be alone," Frank shouted. "It's Patricia who's in hot water, not you."

Wrong, Frank.

"Oh, come on, Frank," I said. "We're all beat. Let's get some sleep and talk later. At least Patricia isn't in jail. They won't charge her. I just know they won't."

Frank mumbled incoherently, like a baby gurgling. The feelings flew right past me.

"It's hard to believe Paul Marks is dead," he said finally, before he hung up.

"I really don't believe it either."

I didn't sleep the next night. I watched the sun rise through the big black palm tree, sending knife-shaped shadows over the patio.

Some men came about ten o'clock, men in blue uniforms and neatly starched little hats. They hauled black hoses through the side alley and snaked them into the pool. I guessed they were cleaning the pool. I felt usurped. I'd always considered the pool to be my domain, my responsibility.

I went into the kitchen, padded across sticky spots on the cheap brown linoleum floor (made to look like tile), ate a bowl of cold cereal with faintly sour milk.

People went up and down the back stairs, voices I could have identified if I tried.

I did not.

When I went back to the living room, my lips rancid with milk, I noticed that the swimming pool was now empty.

The men were gone. The hoses were still there. I imagined the pool would be refilled with black water.

Later, I took a shower. I examined my body. Full veins mapping unblemished skin, the color of caramel. I had been up all night; I should have looked tired, run-down. My body is like the city, I thought, victim of unexplainable moods.

If I ever figure it out, I will be dead.

I wondered how much my counterpart weighed. He was inside me now. I wore him. He wore me. It didn't matter which. We had no need of further exchanges through the mirror. He was a permanent stranger, a perfect resident.

I felt heavy, solid, doubly distilled. I was walking now for two, for three, and more; for everyone I had met or seen.

In the foggy bathroom mirror was a ghostlike reflection, broad shoulders, pale eyes. I was glad, at least, that there was something there. I was almost certain now that the reflection was only the play of light on a silver surface, nothing more. It would have been difficult to explain the empty space in the mirror on social occasions.

Tilting my head up, mouth open, I let the water pour into me.

Water brought back strange memories, stirred up the sediment. Water was essential to my life, like blood to a vampire; allowed me to stay inside, an eternal baptism of self.

Watching the foggy mirror, my body through the fog, I thought: The water that falls about my feet is liquid mirror, down the drain, into the processing plants, then out to sea.

The world is a mirror.

I turned off the shower, suddenly fearing too much of a good thing.

The doorbell was ringing as I stepped out of the tub.

"Damn," I said, "someone's always after me."

Pulling on a sea-blue bathrobe, I went to the door.

Patricia stood back a good distance. I couldn't tell if it was something about me that repelled her or if she felt that I would be repelled by her. Violence could hang about you like a shroud, off-putting and terrible; a part of a person's nature that they, or you, might not want to see; an uncleanness.

"He's dead," I said. She did not move, but stared at my robe as though hypnotized by the color.

"He's dead," she echoed, and walked past me, a faint wind of perfume and worried perspiration.

She knelt on the couch, resting her chin on the window-sill and staring into the yard.

The day was bright, cloudless, the sky a powdery blue.

When she turned around to face me, her eyes were full of love, a mother's eyes, a lover's eyes, the feeling you have about yourself.

"Michael," she said suddenly her voice sweet and yet dark. "Michael, I'm more worried for you than for me."

I went into the kitchen. I poured a cup of coffee, came back in, not knowing what to say. My heart was mute. The more I looked in her eyes, the farther away I was.

She shot from the couch and came at me. I fended her off with my arms, but they moved slowly, stiffly, alienly.

She slipped under them, held me fast. As though she were ill-fitting clothing, I shed her.

"Michael," she said sharply, then struck me with the back of her hand. "Michael, I did it for you."

I looked at her numbly. "Did what?" I said.

"Tried to stop . . . Paul. His influence over you."

"His what?"

She held out a hand, as if offering me a last hope. It was steady, untrembling. I looked at it as though it were a picture of a hand.

"That's nice, Patricia," I said hollowly.

"Apparently it was too late," she said, dropping her empty hand to her side. One thing you could say about Patricia, she knew when to give up.

She walked out the door, not looking back.

The day passed. The sun made its usual arc. When night came, I slept for the first time since the death.

I couldn't say whether it was dream, whether it was reality, or a mixture. But it was as if I were relaxing completely for the first time.

I slept with my eyes open.

The surface of the mirror turned to water, wind-stirred water.

"Come here," it said.

"No," I said. "I thought you were finished with me."

"You are finished with you," it said. "But I am the building and have one more thing to do for you."

There was still some resistance left in me, and I fought the pull. It was too strong. I plunged into the mirror headlong, my feet lingering in my apartment for a moment.

Then I was gone; howling through the walls like a lost child.

As the sun moved over the building, I could feel its blind gaze pounding down, then its retreat. As the sun moved toward the sea, a waterline approached, retreated, leaving a dark signature on the sand.

The shadows lengthened and the backyard turned purple and the leaves a rich dark green.

Inside the walls of the building, I found a deeper sleep, or it found me; silver, swirling. I was pulled under, into clear blue depths, where I could breathe.

I fell, I spiraled, a perfect dark shape, fashioned of seaweed, a rubber bladder filled with water, watching the sea bottom approach with eyes made of seawater and sand.

In the cold depths where no sun reached, there was an abundance of life. The hagfish. Sleeping sharks. Nameless things that burrowed in the sunless sand. The drift of particles from upper, light-filled waters, some living, some not.

When I hit bottom, I sensed movement about me. But I did not look. There was no need.

The ocean, the shadows, the faces: it was all me.

I woke staring at the mirrorless door. Downstairs, I knew, there was a mirror in that space, reflecting strange furniture, the mortal remains of another's life.

I stretched my new body. On my lips I tasted Patricia, Janette, Michael, a score of others.

I spit, and got up heavily. I did jumping jacks, my arms razoring through the air.

Throwing open the blinds, I felt the night close about me like a leather glove. I had slept almost twelve hours, but it was still dark. I looked at the clock, then turned it facedown on the bedstand.

The room was close and I opened the window. A faint salty breeze came in.

I climbed out onto the balcony, running fingers through coarse black hair. My head almost touched the top rail. I had grown inches while I'd slept.

I reached down and stroked the warm shaft of my penis. Hands dangling at my side, I watched myself get an erection, blue in the night light, black-veined.

And smiled.

I looked up. For a moment I saw stars. Then my mind clenched like a fist; and there was only a flat darkness, like black paper, on which I could imagine anything. I imagined shooting holes in that paper, and seeing what would come through.

I went back inside, put on my clothes. I needed. My loins were burning. It was still dark. There was time.

Looking down at the floor, his ceiling, I wondered if they would recognize Michael in my casket.

And how I would explain my presence in the building.

When I got back, I would figure it out; and take care of Patricia for good.

I stretched, contracted, walked out the door. I was myself again, whole, without scars or memory.

Now maybe real life can begin at last.

PLUME

(0452)

THE CONTEMPORARY SCENE

☐ **MEN WHO LOVED ME** *A Memoir in the Form of a Novel* **by Felice Picano.** When Picano returns to Manhattan's West Village, he gets caught up in the gay movement and orgies of drugs, music, and beautiful people, "Zesty . . . a distinguished and humorous portrait of a vanished age."—*Publishers Weekly* (265282—$8.95)

☐ **SHOCKPROOF SYDNEY SKATE A Novel by Marijane Meaker.** It's an erotic adventure that becomes Sydney's hilarious, poignant journey toward adulthood, where love isn't what he expected—and yet it may be so much more than he ever dreamed. (265398—$8.95)

☐ **UNUSUAL COMPANY by Margaret Erhart.** "Graceful . . . convincing and sensitive."—*Booklist* Franny meets Claire in Rizzoli's bookstore, and for weeks this strange, lovely woman becomes her obsession. Beginning a journey of spirit, Franny moves away from her safe existence into Claire's demimonde of dangerous love and exotic violence.... (264421—$9.00)

☐ **THE CATHOLIC by David Plante.** Daniel Francoeur is a young man uneasily aware of his gay sexuality—a sexuality both nurtured and tormented by his passionate religious feelings. This remarkable novel is a brilliant and startlingly honest exploration of spirituality and passion, guilt and eroticism, exegesis and obsession. "Vivid . . . wonderful."—Andrew Holleran, in *Christopher Street* (259282—$7.95)

☐ **SECOND SON by Robert Ferro.** Mark Valerian, the second son in the Valerian family, is ill, but determined to live life to the fullest—and live forever if he can. When he discovers Bill Mackey, a young theatrical designer who is also suffering from the disease neither wants to name, he also finds the lover of his dreams. Together, Mark and Bill develop an incredible plan to survive, a plan which ultimately leads father and son to a confrontation of the painful ties of kinship . . . and the joyous bonds of love. "Eye-opening and stirring."—*The Village Voice* (262259—$8.95)

Buy them at your local bookstore or use this convenient coupon for ordering.

NEW AMERICAN LIBRARY
P.O. Box 999, Bergenfield, New Jersey 07621

Please send me the books I have checked above.
I am enclosing $_____ (please add $2.00 to cover postage and handling).
Send check or money order (no cash or C.O.D.'s) or charge by Mastercard or VISA (with a $15.00 minimum). Prices and numbers are subject to change without notice.

Card # _____ Exp. Date _____

Signature _____

Name _____

Address _____

City _____ State _____ Zip Code _____

For faster service when ordering by credit card call 1-800-253-6476

Allow a minimum of 4-6 weeks for delivery. This offer is subject to change without notice

PLUME

(0452)

COMING OF AGE

☐ **THE SALT POINT by Paul Russell.** This compelling novel captures the restless heart of an ephemeral generation that has abandoned the future and all of its diminished promises. "Powerful, moving, stunning!"—*The Advocate* (265924—$8.95)

☐ **PEOPLE IN TROUBLE by Sarah Schulman.** Molly and her married lover Kate are playing out their passions in a city-scape of human suffering. "Funny, street sharp, gentle, graphic, sad and angry . . . probably the first novel to focus on aids activists."—*Newsday* (265681—$9.00)

☐ **THE BOYS ON THE ROCK, by John Fox.** Sixteen-year-old Billy Connors feels lost—he's handsome, popular, and a star member of the swim team, but his secret fantasies about men have him confused and worried—until he meets Al, a twenty-year-old aspiring politician who initiates him into a new world of love and passion. Combining uncanny precision and wild humor, this is a rare and powerful first novel. (262798—$9.00)

Prices slightly higher in Canada.

Buy them at your local bookstore or use this convenient coupon for ordering.

NEW AMERICAN LIBRARY
P.O. Box 999, Bergenfield, New Jersey 07621

Please send me the books I have checked above.
I am enclosing $_____ (please add $2.00 to cover postage and handling).
Send check or money order (no cash or C.O.D.'s) or charge by Mastercard or VISA (with a $15.00 minimum). Prices and numbers are subject to change without notice.

Card # _____ Exp. Date _____
Signature _____
Name _____
Address _____
City _____ State _____ Zip Code _____

For faster service when ordering by credit card call 1-800-253-6476

Allow a minimum of 4-6 weeks for delivery. This offer is subject to change without notice

Plume

NOVELS OF GENIUS AND PASSION

(0452)

☐ **NIGHTS IN ARUBA by Andrew Holleran.** At the center of this novel is Paul, an uneasy commuter between two parallel lives: one as the dutiful son of aging, upper-middle-class parents, the other as a gay man plunged deliriously into the world of bars, baths, and one night stands. It is a story of love shared and love concealed. (263956—$8.95)

☐ **THREE NIGHTS IN THE HEART OF THE EARTH by Brett Laidlaw.** Bryce Fraser is the precocious younger son of a college professor/poet and his wife. He is about to experience three days in his family's history that will transform his world and theirs. As in Arthur Miller's *Death of a Salesman,* the characters in the Fraser family are both ordinary and heroic . . . and headed toward tragedy. This powerful and moving, exquisitely written family novel reveals an extraordinary fictional talent. "Admirable . . . A narrative that achieves considerable intensity and grace." —*The New York Times Book Review* (262208—$7.95)

☐ **JOB'S YEAR by Joseph Hansen.** Oliver Jewett has reached his fifty-eighth year. It is his time of truth. He must face the present, the lover he feels himself losing, the young man who tempts him so dangerously. This wise and mature novel lays bare the workings of the human heart and of a good man in a troubled territory familiar to us all. (261171—$8.95)

☐ **MONTGOMERY'S CHILDREN by Richard Perry.** "Perry shares Toni Morrison's gifts for psychological as well as pathological insights. The male bonding between Gerald and Iceman is reminiscent of Milkman and Guitar's in *Song of Solomon.* Perry's gift makes him a writer to be savored and watched."—*The Village Voice* (256747—$7.95)

Prices slightly higher in Canada.

Buy them at your local bookstore or use this convenient coupon for ordering.

NEW AMERICAN LIBRARY
P.O. Box 999, Bergenfield, New Jersey 07621

Please send me the books I have checked above.
I am enclosing $_____ (please add $2.00 to cover postage and handling).
Send check or money order (no cash or C.O.D.'s) or charge by Mastercard or VISA (with a $15.00 minimum).
Prices and numbers are subject to change without notice.

Card # _____ Exp. Date _____
Signature _____
Name _____
Address _____
City _____ State _____ Zip Code _____

For faster service when ordering by credit card call 1-800-253-6476

Allow a minimum of 4-6 weeks for delivery. This offer is subject to change without notice